More Praise for *Chiara di Assisi*

"In her passionate book marked by dreams and ongoing questions, Dacia Maraini delivers a gorgeous portrait of Clare of Assisi, who succeeded in giving life to a revolutionary language and overturning the rules of her time in order to follow one rule, her own."

—*Corriere Adriatico*

"This intimate and provocative book is the story of an encounter, between a great woman writer who has made words the very instrument with which she can tell a story about reality, and an intelligent, determined woman to whom the use of the word was denied."

—Enza Cavallaro, *Il Quotidiano di Calabria*

"As with Francis, for Clare the profound significance of poverty is that one has the freedom to invent one's own destiny. With this book, in part an exchange of letters with a mysterious interlocutor, in part a diary, Dacia Maraini has added a precious, missing link to her feminist writings, all the more convincing for its distance from any form of philosophical or political abstraction."

—Emanuele Trevi, *Corriere della Sera*

In Praise of Disobedience

Other Voices of Italy: Italian and Transnational
Texts in Translation

Editors: Alessandro Vettori, Sandra Waters, and
Eilis Kierans

This series presents texts of any genre originally written in
Italian with the aim of introducing new or past authors,
who have until now been marginalized, to an English-
speaking readership. It also highlights contemporary
transnational authors as well as writers who have never
been translated or who were translated in the past but need
a new translation. The series focuses on the translator as a
crucial figure for the dissemination of art and knowledge,
increasing the appreciation of translation as an art form
that enhances cultural diversity.

The present book encompasses many of these qualities.
It was written by one of Italy's most vital, prolific, and
well-known contemporary writers whose work examines
violence against women, sexism, and the struggle for
equality. The book re-evaluates the revolutionary figure
of Saint Clare through correspondence between two
21st-century women, exploring the difficulties women faced
in medieval Italy while emphasizing the freedom the
protagonist attains by virtue of her progressive ideas and
gutsy heart. *In Praise of Disobedience* was one of Maraini's
few books not available in English and its translation was a
labor of love by a scholar of medieval and early modern
Italian literature. Its publication comes during a pandemic
that has–in the spirit of Clare's cloistered nuns–moved
society to see the potential of community and collaboration
for transforming enclosed spaces. Its contents will no doubt
resonate with readers of all backgrounds.

In Praise of Disobedience

Clare of Assisi

DACIA MARAINI

Translated by Jane Tylus

Rutgers University Press

New Brunswick, Camden, and Newark, New Jersey

London and Oxford, UK

Rutgers University Press is a department of Rutgers, The State University of New Jersey, one of the leading public research universities in the nation. By publishing worldwide, it furthers the University's mission of dedication to excellence in teaching, scholarship, research, and clinical care.

Library of Congress Cataloging-in-Publication Data

Names: Maraini, Dacia, author. | Tylus, Jane, 1956– translator.
Title: In praise of disobedience: Clare of Assisi / Dacia Maraini; translated by Jane Tylus.
Other titles: Chiara di Assisi. English | Clare of Assisi
Description: New Brunswick: Rutgers University Press, [2023] | Series: Other voices of Italy | Includes bibliographical references.
Identifiers: LCCN 2022011760 | ISBN 9781978833920 (paperback; alk. paper) | ISBN 9781978833937 (hardback ; alk. paper) | ISBN 9781978833944 (epub) | ISBN 9781978833951 (mobi) | ISBN 9781978833968 (pdf)
Subjects: LCSH: Clare, of Assisi, Saint, 1194–1253—Fiction. | LCGFT: Biographical fiction. | Novels.
Classification: LCC PQ4873.A69 C5513 2023 | DDC 853/.914—dc23/eng/20220513
LC record available at https://lccn.loc.gov/2022011760

A British Cataloging-in-Publication record for this book is available from the British Library.

Published in Italian as *Chiara di Assisi.*
English translation © 2023 Jane Tylus
Foreword © 2023 Rudolph M. Bell
© 2013 RCS Libri S.p.A., Milan
© 2016–2017 Rizzoli Libri S.p.A., Milan
© 2018 Mondadori Libri S.p.A./BUR, Milan

www.rutgersuniversitypress.org

"Such was her mildness and sweetness in admonishing her sisters, and in the other good and holy things that she did, that one's tongue cannot possibly tell of all that was in Lady Clare."
—From the canonization proceedings for Clare of Assisi

Contents

Translator's Preface

I first met Dacia Maraini on a chilly night in New York City—March 13, 2014, to be exact. I know the date because Dacia inscribed it in the copy of *Chiara di Assisi: Elogio della disobbedienza* that she kindly gave me as we were leaving NYU's Casa Italiana following my interview with her about this bracing new book. It was a book that had gotten under my skin as I was reading it in preparation for our meeting. So too does Clare of Assisi herself get under the skin of the novelist or "Cara scrittrice," the writer who is very much a character in her own book and who finds herself increasingly caught up in the Middle Ages despite her best intentions. I had the opposite experience, in some ways. Dacia lured me out of my academic fixation on the Middle Ages and into the present, enabling me to work on a contemporary text for a change. How refreshing to be in contact with the author whose book you are translating and, in Dacia's case, someone who is always responsive to your every question, eager to hear your own thoughts; someone for whom a book is, truly, never closed.

The novelist as vulnerable, compassionate, and, in a less ethical register, curious about the world around her, its past and its possible futures, and especially its varied and always unsettling present. This is the posture that Dacia occupies in *Chiara di Assisi* as in other recent works, as she probes episodes of violence against women, the difficulties of growing up, and unjust uses of power, all while keenly listening for and to the voices of the unchosen. But such discourse is always in the framework of telling a story, the work that writers do, and *Chiara di Assisi* breaks new ground with its experimental form and engaging conversations.

The book you hold in your hands, dear reader, is the product of my own conversation with Dacia—on the page, as well as in person in Rome, Florence, London, and New York. I would like to thank Stefano Albertini for asking me to interview Dacia back in 2014, Renee Zuckerbrot for her editorial advice and support, Michael Moore for his comments on an early version of the work, Alessandro Vettori for his encouragement to submit the translation to the Other Voices of Italy series after he attended my virtual talk on Dacia's book (and Daniela D'Eugenio for inviting me to give the talk in the first place), Eilis Kierans and Sandra Waters for their careful reading of the final manuscript and shepherding it through press, and Dacia for caring so deeply about her readers—and her translators.

Jane Tylus

Foreword

I am honored to offer a brief introduction to this new volume in the Rutgers University Press series dedicated to bringing outstanding Italian literature, contemporary and classic, in translation for Anglophone audiences. The series promises to place the work of the university's distinguished Department of Italian Language and Literature before a wide audience.

The honor is also a pleasure in that the Italian author, Dacia Maraini, and the American translator, Yale University Professor Jane Tylus, bring such talent to their respective endeavors. And by fortuitous coincidence, or maybe not merely coincidence, the terrain upon which their work converges happens to be the *vita* of one of my favorite and yet most elusive saints, Clare of Assisi.

Perhaps the extraordinary range of Dacia Maraini's literary corpus should have prepared me for anything, but, truth be said, I did not clearly foresee the depths of her exploration of such distant territory. Likewise, Jane Tylus's loving expertise on medieval Siena and its heroic Saint Catherine Benincasa did not lead me to anticipate that she would take on the translation of a contemporary author. But here we have it: the splendid result of their collaboration.

The story begins with a not-so-humble letter addressed to the illustrious author Dacia Maraini. It is from Chiara

Mandalà, a mysterious young woman who identifies herself as a resident of the Sicilian village of Santo Pellegrino. The unexpected and unwanted letter boldly requests, even demands, that Maraini set aside her own work to undertake an exploration of the life of the thirteenth-century Saint Clare of Assisi, Chiara's namesake. In some way, however mundane or psychotic, young Chiara expects this knowledge from the remote past to enable her to unearth her present-day buried self-awareness. The dozens of missives the two women exchange over the next few months convey mutually deepening empathy, revealed not only as they share arcane bits of evidence from the *vita* and writings of Saint Clare but also as Dacia Maraini evokes personal encounters, ranging from the untimely death of her companion Giuseppe Moretti to the fashioning of her theatrical portrayal of Saint Catherine of Siena's anorexia.

Then the epistolary comes to an unexpected stop. At the very moment when harried author Maraini finally agrees to immerse herself in the thirteenth-century Saint Clare, the twenty-first-century adolescent Chiara disappears. Upon investigation, Maraini finds that even the name of the lonely child's village is fictitious. Maybe the girl herself does not exist. The illustrious author continues her exploration alone, blending facts, fictions, interpretations, and speculations into a marvelous exposition on medieval European women's dreams and desires, always with a conscious grounding in contemporary feminism and the oppressions of male sexual dominance. Oh, how I envy her liberation from the arrogant constraints and restrictive norms of academic scholarship. Let poetic license reign supreme as it unleashes its own truths!

At one level, the better-documented aspects of the lives of Saint Clare and of her senior partner Saint Francis do not offer much promise as inspiration for Maraini's feminist ideals. Famously, he stripped himself naked in broad daylight before a large crowd in Assisi's busy market square, gathered to witness his rebellion against his father, Pietro Bernardone dei Moriconi. By contrast, she had to settle for being tonsured secretly at Francis's hand in the darkness of night at his tiny, remote Porziuncola chapel. His dramatic conversion to a new way of life came after more than a decade devoted to wine, women, and rowdy song. Her escape from the comforts of home and eventual marriage came after an innocent adolescence marked by deep spiritual devotion, much in the mold of her blessed mother, Ortolana Fiumi. In the years that followed, Francis adventured into the woods outside Gubbio to confront and tame a ravenous man-eating wolf, whereas Clare humbly enclosed herself in convent walls for her remaining forty years, where she wove garments with which to clothe her clerical superiors. He chose not to enter the priesthood, saying he felt unworthy of the honor that came with performing the miracle of transforming ordinary bread and wine into the body and blood of Christ. She had no choice about her absolute exclusion from the ranks of Christ's most honored followers. He wandered about much of central Italy, preaching before large crowds, whether of birds, people, or fish. She was denied all public voice, and it is only through a handful of letters to the similarly enclosed Saint Agnes of Prague that we have meaningful access to her thoughts. A twenty-first-century pope took Francis as his namesake. Clare will receive no such recognition.

The process by which Maraini inverts the negativity of these historical realities begins with a suggestion from the pushy Sicilian adolescent Chiara Mandalà in her next-to-last missive in the initial phase of their correspondence: "I'd like to figure out how to stop fasting, but that will happen only if I can manage to possess a happy body. You set forth the hypothesis that Clare's body wasn't a happy one, notwithstanding the extreme joy she knew from spiritual ecstasy. What makes you think this—her sickness? And what if even that was a way of affirming an iron will, of subjecting her body to her spirit?" Enticingly and powerfully, Maraini encourages us to consider, as Clare and her holy sisters have done through the ages, illness as conquest of the female body sculpted by men, enclosure as walling off male intrusiveness, silence as defiance against authoritarian commands, absolute poverty as rejection of masculine definitions of success, and virginity as the ultimate "no" in response to Adam's request for a helpmate of his own flesh, one over whom he would exercise dominion forever.

We drift briefly and more openly from historical reality, as Maraini invokes a fifteenth-century artistic representation of Clare standing next to a portrayal of Francis with stigmatic wounds, chronologically implausible since by 1224 she had been cloistered for over ten years, and yet rich with interpretive insights. In language that on occasion may cause readers to respond, "How disgusting!" the author then sets before us testimonies from canonization proceedings undertaken less than two years after Clare's death in 1253, blending the distant memories of aging nuns with the timeless physical realities well known to lowly third-world hospital cleanup crews. We are introduced to the gritty details of daily life in a rustic convent where the women lacked sufficient running water to cleanse themselves and often went hungry, voluntarily or not: soiled backsides, infestations of lice, muddy feet, dirty linens, putrid drinking water. All these torments and many more, Clare steadfastly "transformed into rapture."

As the weeks and months roll by on Maraini's twenty-first-century calendar, scholarly bibliographic references increasingly give way to dream sequences, allowing the author to transport us ever more deeply into Saint Clare's most intimate, omnitemporal meditations. A turn of the page brings us to autobiographical recollections from Maraini's teenage days at Florence's Santissima Annunziata boarding school for elite girls, where she overcame nightly bouts of insomnia by seeking refuge in Christ's crucified body, memories that opened her sensibilities to oneness with enclosed women across the ages. There follows a lengthy parade of thoughts and anxieties drawn from a pantheon of female mystics, mostly Italian and in the Catholic tradition, remarkable for their capacious openness to our individual reflections as readers—male and female, young and old, believer and skeptic, Anglophone and not.

Already you may have guessed the ending of this evocative journey, at least in part. The Sicilian adolescent girl Chiara Mandalà returns, making a grand entrance I shall leave for author Dacia Maraini and translator Jane Tylus to reveal.

—Rudolph M. Bell
Distinguished Professor of History Emeritus,
Rutgers University

Postscript

Rudy Bell was renowned not only for his profound scholarship and knowledge of his specific field, Medieval and Renaissance Italy, but for his striking humility and wisdom. His warm presence, sharp intellect, and wit resonated with all who had the chance to cross paths with him. Rudolph M. Bell was Distinguished Professor Emeritus of the Department of History at Rutgers, known to everyone simply as Rudy, always available to mentor students and young colleagues or simply to offer advice to anyone who asked. We are deeply thankful for having known him in his various capacities as friend and advocate of the Italian Department at Rutgers, but we are especially grateful for the privilege of publishing one of his last pieces on a topic that was so dear to him, medieval women saints.

In Praise of Disobedience

Dear Author,

I'm a student from Sicily who lives in a tiny little village called Santo Pellegrino on the slopes of Mt. Etna. It's at the far end of this impoverished but beautiful island—an island you know well, and one that I love, although I always feel its flaws gnawing at me like starving fleas.

My name is Chiara. It's a name that may mean nothing to you, but for me it's really a lot, possibly everything. For a long time, this luminous, crystalline name, a name that speaks with pensive radiance, has been driving me crazy. The choice was simple, almost banal; my pious mother wanted to name me Clare because I was born on the day when we celebrate the saint, August 11—the day she died, since we don't know the date of her birth, or even the year, exactly; perhaps 1193 or 1194.

The banality of coincidences. If I'd been born on the feast day of Saint Genevieve, would my unlucky mother have named me Genoveffa? Blame it on the calendar, I'd say. The fact is that my father wanted to name me after his mother, Giuseppina—a name that made my mother want to vomit. I feel the same way. So to pacify my mother they agreed to name me after the saint on whose feast day I was born. Does this seem remotely serious to you? In the end I'm the result of

1

a compromise. A nice solution, huh? I'm someone who has always felt compromises like knives digging into my flesh.

For years I've been asking myself who I am, because I honestly don't know. That's why I've started with my name, hoping you might help me figure things out. A few months ago I took the train to Assisi. During the trip I read a little book about the saint that I found in our village library. We're poor, as you might have guessed: my father is a contractor, who built some awful, illegal homes on the side of a hill that, when it rains, tend to slide down into the valley. And so he was reported to the authorities. But it wasn't his fault. He built them on behalf of a certain gentleman—though to call him a "gentleman" is a bit of a stretch. So let's just say this man is one of those types who wanted to save the money it would have cost to hire a real architect, who would have forced him not only to pay more but to submit his project to the town council for approval, the kind of thing he'd never done. And in the end, all the blame was laid on my poor, timid father.

My mother is half illiterate, a girl from town who thought she'd made it big by marrying this modest, homely man of peasant stock, a man who learned with considerable effort how to draw lines on a piece of paper, how to count, and how to work with bricks and mortar. The "gentleman," however, who enabled us to survive for years—until they convicted my father of illegal construction, fining him and sending him to jail for four months—owned rural properties that he succeeded in getting "rezoned" for residential purposes with the help of a friend who was a town commissioner. He built lots of illegal apartment buildings, but right before the authorities put a stop to it, he sold them off for a small fortune and with the proceeds bought an enormous shopping mall. Then he turned around and sold that too. He transferred all his money to Romania, where he now runs a big furniture factory. The blame for the illegal construction fell on my father. His name is Alfio, just so you know. He's a good father, in the sense that he's supportive and doesn't ask questions. He let me continue my studies and he doesn't beat his wife, like other men in the village. He has big, blue, innocent eyes and is always sad. In short, I love him.

The city of Assisi filled me with wonder. Maybe it's because I instantly saw it through the pages of the book that I'm reading, a historian's imaginative way of reinventing the Middle Ages. Steep, winding roads, mules and horses climbing up and down, palaces with heavy metal doors, huts built with wood and bricks, huge, elegant churches. But no sooner had those mules set off, their hooves clattering on the stones, than I felt as though I was in a Pasolini film. The cobblestoned streets were no longer out of reach. They were right beneath my feet. The austere narrow towers rose up before my eyes, the ancient houses with their massive walls so close I could rest my hand on them and feel the stones sweating. When I heard a window opening above my head, instinctively I got out of the way, knowing that none of these houses had bathrooms, not even the wealthiest ones. People would urinate into chamber pots that a servant woman quickly emptied out into the middle of the street the next morning. But wait, I asked myself, weren't there sewers? I was remembering Boccaccio's tale from the *Decameron* about Andreuccio of Perugia who tumbled into a dark well in Naples. But it doesn't mean that you could access the black holes of sewers through the bedroom. Did people have latrines in their homes? I'll have to figure that one out. . . . I saw mules laden down with wood, making their way up the hills just like they do in my village, climbing those impassable streets. I saw the shops of thirteenth-century Assisi, with jars in some windows and piles of fabric stacked up in others.

But I'll stop here because I don't want to bore you. I would be so happy if you wrote me back. You're the only one who can help me understand these things. I understand nothing.
Yours, Chiara Mandalà

Dear Chiara,
What an odd letter. But I'm the one who must ask you something—what do you want from me? You tell your story with intelligence and spirit, but where do you want it to lead? I know nothing about Saint Clare, nor do I want to. Explain yourself more clearly.
Regards, DM

Dear Author,
I was so happy to get your answer I started dancing! I thought you'd just ignore me. I confess (and if we start getting to know each other you'll learn that my need to tell the truth always drives me to bang my head against the wall), I confess that before turning to you, I wrote to another writer with the same request. He never answered me. And then, out of the depths of my memory came the images of eighteenth-century Palermo, its uneven streets and carriage wheels constantly rumbling and ringing in the ears of the townspeople all day long and maybe even all night. I remembered your book on Marianna Ucrìa and I realized in a flash that I had approached the wrong writer. The right person is you. Please forgive me if I didn't write to you first, but only after I failed to hear anything back from the other famous writer from my island!

What do I want from you? It's not easy to explain. But I swear, I'm not looking for an introduction to an editor, or for you to write a preface to a book, or to be propelled into the world of literature. I have no literary ambitions. What I would like is for you to join me on this journey into memory, in search of a woman who's no longer here. That's how I see myself: nameless and invisible, although I do have a name and an address and even a family, disgraced though it is. I've become passionate about the story of Clare of Assisi, but why that's so isn't yet clear to me. I'd like you to help me understand. I do know that the more I learn about my namesake, the more extraordinary she seems. To put it bluntly, I want you to write something about the Clare of 800 years ago so you can help me understand something about the Chiara of today. Am I asking too much?

Dear Chiara,
You certainly are a strange creature. You're dragging me into something that doesn't interest me in the least. Why don't *you* write the life of St. Clare? I'm sure you'd do a wonderful job.

Dear Author,
I read something in an interview with you that really struck me. You said that your characters come to visit you. They knock on your door, come in, sit down, and tell you their story. You offer them tea, sometimes with biscotti flavored with licorice. You listen patiently to their stories and then you walk them to the door. Off they go, these characters with their tales, and you never see them again. But then you added something: "Every now and then after drinking my tea and eating my cookies, a character will ask to stay for dinner, and after dinner ask to spend the night, and the next morning ask to have breakfast so as to pick up the story from where it left off the night before. That's when I know it's time to start a new novel."

I know I'm being presumptuous, but I really do feel that this time I'm the one who's knocking at your door and asking you to tell a story, trying to lure you into writing something on Clare. But be forewarned: I won't settle for just tea and lemon or anise biscuits. I also want dinner and a bed for the night.

Dear Chiara,
It's true that I wrote those words, but you are not a character telling me your story. You're proposing the story of someone who is not you, who lived 800 years ago, about whom you know very little, and I know nothing. Why don't you ask a historian? I do know that there's a vast selection of literature on this saint from Assisi who was close to Francis, the patron saint of Italy. I'm certain you'll find an attentive and understanding listener. Now that I think about it, I remember having read some years ago a beautiful book by Chiara Frugoni that talks about the saint from a nonreligious, historical perspective. Why don't you ask her?

Dear Author,
My aspirations may seem excessive to you. My real hope—and I tell you this with my usual frankness—is to dwell inside a happy body. Someone once called my voice "Callas-esque." That's another reason I sought you out; I understand that you knew Maria Callas, and I would like to hear you talk about her. Even though my father gave me permission to keep going to school, after he was denounced for illegal buildings, after all the money spent on lawyers, after the verdict that got him imprisoned for four months, he had only enough money left for me to take singing lessons. They just have an elementary school here in Santo Pellegrino, and for years I'd been putting in four hours a day on the bus, every day, to go back and forth to school. I would get up at five A.M. and come back at seven in the evening. I had to give up on college because it would have meant renting an apartment in the city.

For the moment I have an arrangement with a former opera singer who's eighty years old, the grandmother of a school friend of mine who gives me lessons now and then. She's somewhat absentminded but very sweet. She sang on the stage, though only as a member of the chorus, never as a soloist. But she knows her music and she's helping me study.

Dear Chiara,
I'm understanding you even less: if your vocation is singing, why do you want me to write about Saint Clare? And why put me in the middle of all this—I who am so far removed from saints?

Dear Author,
You'll see that I'm capable of surprising you all over again. I'm a girl who's full of surprises. Not for my beauty; I confess there's nothing glamorous about my looks. I'm shorter than average, with skinny arms, almost no breasts, and the legs of a chicken. I hobble around on those fashionable stilts that pass for high heels; I persist in wearing them even though I know how awful I look. I have the face of a little girl who's eternally surprised and a bit sad. Maybe that's why I attract the attention of men, or maybe it's for my androgynous looks. I'm so thin that I'm filled with tenderness for myself when I'm alone. I do have a nice voice, though it's a little throaty. Don't think I'm being vain, or that I have ridiculous pretensions; I'm just telling you the truth. I'm just as proud of my voice as I'm ashamed of my height and my little-girl body.

My teachers said they liked my voice too. At La Scala in Milan, I placed third in a national competition for young opera singers. Right in front of me is a certificate that says, "Third prize in the National Competition *La Madonnina* goes to Chiara Mandalà for her lyrical soprano voice, with its intense and surprisingly powerful tones." Notwithstanding my height or my androgynous body, people liked the way I sang. But it all ended there. They invited me to continue studying, although I was obviously expected to pay for lessons. And where was I going to find the money for that?

Dear Chiara,
You describe yourself in such an odd manner, almost in a literary fashion. Are you proposing a story to me?

Dear Author,
Don't be so suspicious. Trust me. You have to believe me: I'm not a parasite or an opportunist. I treasure my voice and I'd like you to find something to value in it too. But above all, I'm a girl who doesn't trust herself, who looks in the mirror and constantly asks her reflection, "Who are you anyway? Where did you come from? What are you supposed to be doing in this stupid world, you stupid girl?" And when I don't find an answer, I turn elsewhere, distraught.

My friends tell me I can sometimes come across as silly. But I'm not: it's true, I may be ingenuous, perhaps excessively so. But this naïveté, though it may seem strange to you, gives me strength. I would never have had the courage to write you if I wasn't as naïve as a babe in the woods—"fino alla babberia," as they say around here.

I know my voice, but I don't know myself. And I think that you're the one who can help me. You can help me get to the bottom of this name that weighs me down, to the point of insisting that I take on responsibility for its history. I have this strange feeling that if I can find out who Saint Clare was, I can discover who I am too. The more I read about her, the more amazed I am by the ties that bind us, beyond just our name. There's something desperate and tumultuous about her life and, while I'm keenly aware of all the differences between us, and with all due respect for her sanctity, about mine as well. Does my interpretation of a great saint seem inappropriate to you?

Clare fasted. I fast too. Until now I'd always thought that my refusal to eat came from the hatred I directed to my body. But why should one hate one's own body? Only because it doesn't correspond to accepted canons of beauty? Then, after I read the experts, it occurred to me that I was fasting so I could have one of those athletic little bodies that look like those butterflies you see in the fashion pages. They say that this has happened to so many girls that some fashion houses have started avoiding using really thin models so as not to encourage this practice of enforced dieting. Bulimia—let's just say it straight out. Because you have to eat something, if only so they don't carry you off to the hospital in a straitjacket. But then, as lots of girls taken over by this passion know better than I, you just lock yourself up in the bathroom to throw up. I got really good at doing that. One finger down your throat and everything comes up with great celerity. I like that word, celerity. It sounds a bit dated, doesn't it? Well, from a certain point of view, I'm feeling quite dated myself.

Do you know what made me stop regurgitating everything I ate? Not my mother's recriminations, not the terrorized looks my father threw in my direction, not the fact that I stopped having my periods or that my hair started falling out or that I began losing my sight, not the fact that my legs became so thin they looked like a skeleton's and made me terrified of myself. It was the smell. I stopped because the stench of my vomit would rise up into my nostrils and linger there all day long, like an indelible curse. To the point where I would cry. I would cry and I would vomit. Then I'd rinse my face. But the smell, dear Author, it never went away. It was the stench of my soul, don't you see? The stench of an unhappy body that continued to belong to me even as I disowned it, time and time again.

Clare fasted. So did many mystics after her. I read your play on Catherine of Siena and how when she was thirty-three, the same age as Christ when he died, she starved herself to death. And when the nuns would bring her some salad greens just so she'd survive, she would swallow them so as not to disappoint her sisters. But afterwards she'd slip outside into the garden and, inserting a tiny olive branch down her throat, she'd expel that pitiful little meal they had lovingly prepared for her. I ask myself what Saint Catherine did to overcome her disgust with that smell that covers you like another layer of skin. And in any case, your story about the saint made me think that maybe at the end of the day, this rejection of food on the part of so many women and girls is a demand for a spiritual life.

Dear Chiara,
You're certainly a strange creature! I still don't understand why you're turning to me. Even if you were honest about confessing that you had first tried another writer who paid no attention to you. Just like your mother when she gave you your name, you've thrown yourself to chance: if one author doesn't answer you, you try another one and then another, until the fool who happens to be on duty responds and you pull all the strings—is that how it is?

Dear Author,
No, it's nothing like that. Even though it might seem that way. But there's no need for me to cite Pirandello to show that things are more contradictory and complicated than we think. Behind the mask we all wear, there's another one, and then another, like those Russian dolls nestled one inside

the other. I'm looking for the voice of a writer. It may be an act of mad presumption, insofar as what one person says and another writes can never coincide. But believe me, I'm being sincere, absolutely sincere. What I want beyond any doubt is to find an honest interlocutor. Someone who wants to journey with me into an ancient yet most modern story. A story that could help me but also, and I'm sure of this, you. Why don't we give it a try?

Dear Chiara,
Up until now you've spoken mostly about yourself. I can see that yours is a mortifying story, but what can I do? Aren't you hiding behind Saint Clare in order to pressure me into writing about you, Chiara Mandalà?

Dear Author,
Clare was a virgin; I'm a virgin. Not because I've taken a vow of chastity or to obey some law of the Church, but rather for want of sexual appetite and maybe even pure boredom. Sex seems unwieldy and predictable to me and love an unattainable dream.

Clare invoked a rule of silence, and I live in a world of silence. I'm not good at speaking to anyone. The voices here bounce off the black stones that the flowing lava left behind, and as they harden, they slide into new streets made of asphalt. But they're voices that make no sense. I haven't succeeded in finding anyone who speaks in a meaningful way. That's why I've turned to writers. Did you know Vincenzo Consolo? A writer I loved for his mysterious and lyrical way of immersing himself in his stories. I enjoyed listening to his narrative voice, following him inside his linguistic circumlocutions and his mental labyrinths, and I fell in love. And I'll admit, I wrote to him before I wrote to you, but I think he was already ill by then. I'm sure that had he felt better he would have answered me. A little while ago I learned that he had died. Do writers speak? No, writers write. It's not the same thing. But their writing has a rhythm to it, like music. And when you recognize it, it fills up your ears like some nutritious juice, and the rhythm speaks to you.

Dear Chiara,

I understand, or at least I'm trying to understand your reasoning. But I'm not convinced. What can I do for you? I don't want to chalk you up as a charity case. I don't like that. Even if there's something of the do-gooder in me that prompts me to stretch out my hand whenever I'm faced with a request for help—from whomever it comes. But I think you deserve more than that.

Dear Author,

I only want you to help me think about things. For example, doesn't it seem strange to you that at nineteen I'm still a virgin? My friends consider me eccentric. To my ears, that sounds like a good thing. It goes along with my sense of modesty—a word that seems lost in the meanderings of time. What does it mean, really? To cover oneself up when other girls are exposing themselves? Or to jealously preserve one's sense of dignity; to refuse to play the game of allurement and entrapment? I watch girls my age putting on makeup, dressing up—or rather, undressing—wiggling their hips, speaking in high-pitched voices, all just to find a boy to rub up against and kiss. A friend of mine used to talk to me all the time about kissing: infinite sweetness and painful, secret pleasures. To me such kisses seem obscene. Not because I'm a moralist, believe me, but I see in it all a hypocrisy that's disheartening. Two bodies thrown together by the crass and stupid desire to procreate, don't you see? Isn't this why they couple? They pretend to love each other, they set up house together, and then the troubles begin. He feels like he's in prison, she feels neglected. He sets out to find other lovers, she learns to contain her jealousy and discovers the meaning of frustration. He takes up with a mistress, she pretends not to know anything about it. After a while a baby arrives and they seem happy. But by now erotic weariness has divided them forever, rendering them the accomplices of a monstrous matrimonial convenience comprised of habit, silence, blackmail, and falling out of love. For me it's nothing but cannibalism. They want to tear each other to pieces and eat each other up.

Dear Chiara,
You're running way too fast. You go on reasoning like a train that's been unleashed on a deserted track. But watch out—it's not easy driving a vehicle like that. There's always the risk of losing control and running off the rails.

Dear Author,
Clare chose absolute poverty. She abandoned her beautifully furnished room, a comfortable marriage, a house with fireplaces ablaze, dresses of brocade, jewels, sumptuous cuisine, the affection of her family—all this to go off and live in a shack in the cold, to sleep on a sack stuffed with leaves and spread out on a frigid floor, relying on only a little bit of food offered as alms. I didn't choose poverty. But I've suffered through it. I hold no grudge against my father just because he never learned how to make himself rich. I accepted poverty almost as though it were a virtue. And this is how I recognize myself in Clare of Assisi. Perhaps there's no merit in accepting the poverty one already knows, but at

least I don't live with that anxiety about possessions that so many of my classmates have. An anxiety that's also about erotic possession—and so this obsession with kisses. Kissing inside a car parked on a narrow dead-end street. Kissing in the school bathroom, in the corner of a highway rest stop, behind a door, on the school bus. Don't you think that kissing has become a fetish these days? From a kiss one moves on to rape. That's what my girlfriends from school used to tell me. Even so they keep themselves rooted to those kisses. They dream about them. They mythologize them. And after they kiss they have to jump over a ditch, and often fall in—a ditch of freezing, stagnant water. A ditch where one loses the joy of living. The ditch of humiliation.

Dear Chiara,
But why do you consider love with such profound disgust? And when you're only nineteen? Doesn't this all seem to be— well, a bit pedantic? You're being melodramatic. Forgive me if I say it outright. It's not that I don't believe you, but it seems to me that you're theatricalizing your unease in the world, making it more dramatic and more literary than it really is. Why compare yourself to a saint from the thirteenth century? Why blame all of history in order to talk about an illness that's totally Italian and common to all your peers? Is it not something that affects every generation as it deals with growing up and tries to make a place for itself in the world of work and passion?

Dear Author,
You're right; perhaps I am being melodramatic. Yes, maybe I'm drawing a sword and waving it about in the air as though I were a woman warrior from the Middle Ages. But can I

tell you something? If my imagination weren't keeping me company, I'd be dead by now. Dead from hunger, for sure. Dead from boredom. Dead because, despite everything else, death seems to me the most surprising, most mysterious, most vibrant part of life itself.

This is why I continue to pursue you, notwithstanding the risk of shocking and boring you. Okay, I'm bookish; I fill myself up with books. One book after another. I can't stop; they're like eating cherries. Listen, I found the book you mentioned to me a little while ago: it's called *An Inhabited Solitude: Clare of Assisi*, by Chiara Frugoni. I devoured it in a single breath. You're right: she writes as though she's squeezing the very juice out of things. It's extraordinary. But it wasn't enough for me. So I went to the library and found other books about the saint: *Francis and Clare of Assisi* by Cesare Vaiani, *The Little Flowers of St. Clare* by Piero Bargellini, *The Complete Writings of Saint Francis and Saint Clare of Assisi* by Chiara Augusta Lainati.

There are so many books, all lying on my bed. I greedily go from one to the next. And yet I feel that the more I read, the less I know about her. What do we know of the Middle Ages? What do I, some poor fool from Santo Pellegrino, what do I know about that epoch, primitive, cruel, and yet glorious though it was? But I'll pack up these books and send them to you. I want *you* to read them. I can't close my eyes as they ransack the pages. Why should a girl of eighteen fall in love with poverty and leave her parents' home to grapple with hunger and cold? Why should she cut off her hair—I imagine her golden, curly, splendid hair dropping to the ground beneath the sharp scissors of the Poor Man of Assisi. Why did Clare fall in love with that young man whose ears spread out from his face like fans, a man called Francis?

Dear Chiara,

For heaven's sake, don't send me all those books. And aren't they from your library? I would have to send them back right away with a thousand excuses. In any case, my house is already groaning under the weight of books. Soon things will fall out just like they do in Ionesco's *Amedeo*—do you know this play? It seems to me that you're a passionate reader, the kind that editors and owners of bookstores like to call "hard-core." Have you ever been interested in theatre? Ionesco recounts the tale of a mysterious corpse that's lying on a bed. With the passing of time, it starts to grow, along with its nails and hair, and it eventually becomes gigantic. That's my idea about books: they seem to be dead, but they're endowed with life itself. Like Ionesco's cadaver, their nails and hair grow too, infinitely expanding their bodies and eventually taking up all the space in your house. Before long, I'll have to get out of there myself so that I can make more room for my books. Do you know I must have almost 10,000 of them, many of them piled up on the floor since there are no more shelves where I can toss them?

Dear Author,

I know I'm being impertinent; I know. But I'm begging you to have a little more patience. I'm knocking at your door, a lowly character in search of I don't even know what, but it's something that makes my head spin and leaves me aghast. I, Chiara from Santo Pellegrino, a tiny town in the Madonie; I, Chiara, with no talent and no prospects; I, Chiara, confined to a humiliating, solitary life; I, Chiara, a lazy virgin, an aching dreamer; I, Chiara, a "hard-core" reader as you yourself put it, ravaged and torn up by all these thoughts: I humbly ask you to consider my offer.

Dear Chiara,

I'm really having trouble understanding your reasoning. I realize you're not happy. I can see that you've found in a faraway Clare the dazzling lights of a mirror that's blurry but inviting. I understand that you want to put into motion some work of writing that could turn out to be anything, as long as it does its job. But what can I do for you? Right now I have another story in mind, and I'm working on a novel set in a period that's light years away from the one you want me to get to know and touch with my hands. Try writing me back in a few months.

Dear Author,

In all sincerity, I have to tell you that Saint Clare can't wait: she's had your tea, but now she wants a bed to sleep in. She's camping out in the home of your imagination and wants to be listened to. I beg you, don't chase us away. I'm holding by the hand an extraordinary woman who has too often been forgotten, neglected, ignored by our country's official history. All the books that I've mentioned to you are published by a single press, Casa Porziuncola of Assisi. But who reads books published by the Porziuncola Press besides scholars of the Middle Ages? And so I tell you with shameless sincerity, if it weren't for Clare of Assisi, we would all be more vulgar and more alone. Without Clare we wouldn't have this other Italy, an Italy of civilized passions and a tradition of poverty chosen with the freedom of one's heart.

My body knows this intimately. But I'd like my awareness to become words, told to others. That's what I'm hungry for. I'm hungry for a story.

Dear Chiara,

I've received your books. Thank you. But I sent them back to the library. I told you I can't comply with your request.

And besides, I insist: why do you want *me* to tell this story of Clare? Among other things, the Middle Ages are quite remote. I know almost nothing about them, save from what I've learned in a few books by historians—Huizinga's *Waning of the Middle Ages*, which I enjoyed reading when I was sixteen. In the meantime, I've read some things by Jacques Le Goff and Georges Duby and our own Franco Cardini. I studied Trotula and her work in medieval medicine when a friend, Giustina Laurenzi, asked me to comment on her nice documentary about the medical school of Salerno.

But now that I think of it, I did once read a book that made me quite curious about the Beguines, a term that's funny in and of itself insofar as it was used to deride those women who were too "bigoted." Instead, I discovered that these scandalized Beguines were often the widows of soldiers killed in battle, who devoted themselves to taking care of the poor; they practiced poverty, chastity, and solidarity, yet without taking official vows. It was the Church that started ridiculing them when their numbers began to swell and they were thought to be influencing public opinion with their virtuous actions and their critiques of the papacy's pomp and authoritarianism.

I might like to write a book on the Beguines, or rather on a single Beguine—Immacolata, Genoveffa, Anastasia, or simply Marietta, who lost her husband to the Crusade, along with her home and eventually her children when they went off into the world. She decided to band together with other women to create a community that wasn't religious but simply based on urban, communal life. They all took turns cooking and washing dishes, working in the garden, weaving cloth to sell, opening a modest school for the children of peasants. That's what the Beguines did. Thank you, Chiara, for bringing me closer to the Middle Ages and for helping me find in their darkness a serene, intelligent, and generous woman like a Beguine.

Dear Author,
So now you realize that I didn't make a mistake by knocking at your door. And you're going to write a book on the Beguines? Rather, on a single Beguine with a kind heart and busy hands? But don't you realize that Clare was a bit of a Beguine? In the sense that she was always the first to perform humble tasks in the convent, like washing and ironing the clothes—just think of those heavy iron bars full of burning coals, and how she would bend down over the cloth, her forehead sweating, careful that a spark didn't fly out and land on the black veils her sisters wore. But now that I think about it, it's likely that they didn't iron in the convent of San Damiano. What would they have ironed? Linens, which I don't imagine they used, while they wore only a tunic of rough wool tied at the waist with a thin cord. Do you think they wore underwear? At the very least, in that cold, they must have needed something on underneath, don't you think? Yes, in fact, they called them drawers, and they were made from coarse cloth, and they washed them about once a week. I don't think they needed ironing. Maybe when it got cold the nuns would put on underclothes that they made for themselves in the convent from raw wool.

Don't run away from me now that I've made you curious. Don't abandon me! I'm ready to bring you some other books that will help you understand that difficult and contradictory epoch, so devoted to excess, so capable of dreaming big, so cruel to its enemies and affectionate with its friends. Let the Beguines wait, I beg you. Dedicate just a little more of your time and attention to our Clare who's waiting.

Dear Chiara,

Actually, I'm in the middle of writing a novel about a love affair. It's very hard to talk about love, don't you think? You've interrupted me with all this furious knocking. I truly don't know whether I should be upset with you or grateful. But for now I'll sign off with affection.

Yours, DM

Dear Author,

I was thinking that this time you'd have really sent me packing. And it would have been a crime. After having awakened our willful little Clare of Assisi, why abandon her?

Lately I've been dreaming about her every night. And I'm sure that within a few months she'll start showing up in your dreams as well. I think that Clare was almost diabolically stubborn. That meager, graceful body possessed a will of steel. She's captured me with her ironclad fingers and holds me tight without touching me, through the sheer magnetism of her deep blue eyes, her fierce and decisive bearing, her voice like that of a baby bird fallen from its nest. In fact, Clare didn't talk at all. It was forbidden to speak in the convent. And when the nuns wanted to communicate among themselves, they did so with gestures. Can you imagine Sister Clare indicating through gestures that a pot had to be filled? Or that a rosary had to be picked up from the ground? I'm sure they all obeyed her without grumbling because she was the first to dedicate herself to lowly tasks and because, as her biographers say, she was always patient, loving, gentle, a "humble virgin."

Isn't it odd how among all these adjectives they include virginity as though it were an aspect of her character and not a choice? Humble and virginal, gentle and virginal, patient and virginal. What does that mean? And why should a saint have to be a virgin, untouched by a man's hands? Is that what virginity is? Doesn't sensuality have a life all its own, apart from other bodies? Autoeroticism, for example: doesn't that constitute a body's sexuality? And how many Christian martyrs, how many saints were married before they dedicated themselves to God? Would we want to maintain that their sanctity and martyrdom are less precious because they were no longer virgins? We don't require men to be virgins. Does never having made love to a woman make a man a virgin? Masculine virginity is considered to be less important because there's no way to physically prove it, there's no hymen to be ruptured. But isn't sexuality something more complex, more far-reaching and profound than the physical act of coupling?

Dear Chiara,
I've never really understood all of this business about virginity either, unless you consider it from the historical point of view. Virginity guarantees the transmission of inheritance; that much I can understand. It is tied closely to the origins of property. The need to control the fertility of one's life companion, the need to have a biological guarantor for one's family possessions. This I can understand. But the myth of virginity in and of itself is incomprehensible. As you say, if sexuality involves the entire body, one's personality, even one's thoughts, then how can virginity possibly matter? As Hume writes, knowledge is attained through the senses, and among the senses we must include eros. What does spirituality have to do with an intact hymen?

Dear Author,
And yet among the attributes of female saints, virginity was important.

Dear Chiara,

Don't forget, I'm a layperson and I don't believe in sanctity. What, after all, is sanctity? Is it making a donkey fly, curing a sick man, observing with amazement a jug left sitting on a boundary wall that's filled itself up with oil? Or bearing in the center of one's hand a tiny wound that recalls the stigmata of Christ? In Africa I knew healers who chased out diseases in the course of lengthy ceremonies, and I once met a woman who told me of having been killed by her husband and then brought back to life, thanks to a holy man who covered her body with boiling ashes and put three cola seeds into her mouth that were a hundred years old.

Dear Author,

I know that you're a layperson. But what does the word "lay" even mean? I'm the one this time to pose the question: Is it opening a window and saying that the world is whatever you see behind that frame? Does being lay only mean that you entrust yourself to the reasons you come up with for something, just like Buridanus's donkey, tempted equally by his hunger and his thirst to choose between a stack of hay and a pail of water, and so condemned to have neither?

Dear Chiara,

What does Buridanus's donkey have to do with anything? Don't you realize you're being pushy? Where have you learned this shameless behavior? You shouldn't be talking about yourself as ingenuous, as you explained it to me a few days ago. I repeat: I know nothing about Clare and I can't possibly take her up now.

Dear Author,

You may not realize it, but you're already caught up in this enchanting narrative. And I've figured out that you've been reading about the saint. Otherwise you wouldn't have spoken of that empty jar resting on the wall that filled itself up with oil. It's one of Clare's little domestic miracles. Those women who lived on alms and walked around in bare feet, but were enclosed inside a convent: how did they manage to beg for alms? That's what the brothers did, the friars, Francis's friends and companions of the street. They did their begging for them. One day, realizing there wasn't a drop of oil in the entire convent, Clare put a jug out on the wall so Friar Leo or Friar Jacob would realize they needed to go out and beg for some oil from houses in the neighborhood. Instead, when the friar on duty picked up the jug, it was heavy, and he discovered that it was full to the brim with fresh, fragrant oil. The touching thing about this is that unlike male saints, female saints perform modest miracles, fit for a convent. Clare multiplies pieces of bread for her sisters' lunch, she heals babies brought to her in their parents' arms, she cures a sick nun who has a fever. It was sufficient that one of her rough little hands—rough, I want to remind you again, because they brandished a broom and rags to wash the floor—it was enough that one of her hands, warm and rough, humble and rough, sweet and rough, charitable and rough, would come to rest on the burning forehead of a sick nun and the fever would take off, legs flying in the air, just like that miniature devil who took on the form of a hairy spider that you have Saint Catherine of Siena describing in your play about the saint. It made me laugh, but with relief. You found that in one of her letters, right?

It's comforting to think that evil takes on recognizable forms: a billy goat with sparkling eyes, a black cat with its tail erect, an ape with an angry sneer, a spider with hairy legs. The imagination made itself at home in the physical makeup of those women locked up for life. While today we've come to the point of believing that evil doesn't have its own body, doesn't have a name or a face. "The banality of evil": isn't that what Hannah Arendt called it? And how can we recognize it? Weren't things easier back then during those days made up of sun and moonlight in which everything took on a precise form under the terrified but credulous eyes of nuns enclosed in a convent? Aren't you touched by this idea of the miraculous in a female monastery in which everything was held in common, including smells, sensations, dreams, and fears? I know that Clare's relationship with poverty is of interest to you. And that you're intrigued by her rapport with Francis. Did you know that Clare was the daughter of nobles of ancient lineage, while Francis belonged to a family of nouveaux riches who imported textiles? His father, Pietro di Bernardone, charged outrageous interest rates from what I've read. He was filthy rich and had his son dressed in the best fabrics, straight from France. Did you know that's why they called him Francis, even though he was baptized Giovanni? Precisely to pay lip service to those textiles he imported from Flanders, so prized by his fellow Italians.

Dear Chiara,

Excuse my delay. But I haven't forgotten you. Something quite unpredictable happened after your last letter. I went to the library to look for a book on Saint Clare. I found a number of them, the very ones that you mentioned to me. In the meantime, I had to go to the United States to speak at a university, and I brought them to read with me on my trip.

And you'll be happy to hear that while I was reading, I realized you were right. Clare speaks to us of an Italy about which we know very little. Not an Italy dismissive of order, but a place profoundly autonomous and mysterious, independent and determined. But the strangest thing is that in the room of an old inn in New Hampshire, in a worm-ridden piece of furniture, I discovered some recently bound books, among which was one on the Middle Ages that talks about St. Clare.

Needless to say, I've been infected. Now I'm immersed in my reading, and little by little I seem to be sliding into an epoch that's very far away—although possibly closer than we think.

Dear Author,

I knew I'd infect you. I knew that you would take Clare's outstretched hand and lead her into the world of the living, just like Orpheus and Eurydice. But remember, don't turn around! Otherwise Clare will be sucked back into the realm of shadows. And instead she deserves to return here among us, with her sickly body, her head full of thoughts, her timid but determined feet. Bare feet even in the winter, on those frigid stones. In Assisi the temperature can drop below fifteen degrees in January and February. Calluses grow on bare feet, and then, just like the paws of a dog, they're no longer sensitive to heat or cold. Do calluses turn into shoes? I see Clare racing along after she's found out that one of the nuns has a high fever. Could it have been her sister Caterina, who when she entered the convent took the name of Agnes? (Was it Saint Francis who gave her that name?) I see Clare rushing toward the room where her little sister lies on her straw sack spread out on the ground. As she's running, she steps on cat poop. There were cats in the convent; the nuns talk about them. Clare stops for an instant to rub her bare foot against some blades of grass that had sprung up between the crumbling tiles. But her foot is still dirty and it leaves dark imprints on the floor. What to do? Does she stop running and go back to clean her foot off in the tub in the middle of the courtyard? Or simply crouch down on the ground, clean off her sole with some dry leaves gathered for the occasion, and then make her way to her sister who needs her help? And will a touch of her hand be enough to banish that fever?

Dear Chiara,

But isn't Agnes the one who escaped from home to join her sister in the convent? And she was followed and captured by a group of young men, brothers and cousins and other outraged members of the family, all led by her uncle Monaldo?

Dear Author,

Yes, that's her. She was caught by a rabble of her brothers and cousins who couldn't stand the idea of having another deserter in the family. What would people have said? A beautiful young woman, all ready to be given in marriage to another well-off dynasty in Assisi. How could anyone justify her flight? How to explain that she preferred to bury herself inside a poor convent dressed in rags, rather than honoring the wealth and property of her family name? They grabbed her and beat her up, kicking and punching her while her uncle Monaldo looked on, furious. Head of the family, he was a heavy-handed, primitive man who simply wanted to tie her up like a cut of meat and carry her home to lock her in the cellar and let her languish of hunger and thirst until she repented and became obedient, as all virgins should be. But then, they say, there was a providential intervention, because while six men were holding Agnes down to drag her away, her body became heavy, so terribly heavy that not even the strongest arms in the world could have lifted her. Only then did they decide to give up, frightened away by the will of God—that's what the legend says.

Another little miracle of a little saint, bound in fraternal love to a monk who called himself a "Frate minore" or little brother? The "great ones" were the nobles, the "middling ones" the merchants, and the "minors" were the people—the excluded, the rejected.

Dear Chiara,

Yes, I did read about how Clare's family was passionately attached to her. But only the women. Agnes and then Beatrice, her two youngest sisters, followed her into the convent. And finally so did her mother, Ortolana. All infected by the hunger of Clare's sacrifice. Could it be that poverty represented a way for women to become independent? Clare said that having possessions meant having to rely on something and on someone. Convents received their property through donations and were controlled by Rome. Thus, to have property meant to be controlled. A control that was economic, political, social, psychological, religious, and rigorously masculine. Yet what could the nuns of San Damiano do to keep themselves going?

Dear Author,

That's exactly why Clare was hoping she wouldn't have to subject herself to life in the cloister. Clare's dream was to preach, to do exactly what the Friars Minor did. Clare dreamt of wandering about in her dirty little feet, begging for food when she got hungry, sleeping in the stalls of animals just as Mary, the mother of Christ, had done, covering herself with only a bit of straw.

Dear Chiara,

Maybe she would have gone about on a donkey.

Dear Author,

Maybe so. The donkey is the humblest of domestic animals. It's that way even when someone kicks it. It's ready to warm the tiny body of a baby with its breath.

Dear Chiara,

A *mammolo*—a little baby boy; isn't that what Clare of Assisi called the infant Jesus? And how many times did they bring her a sick *mammolo* whom she cured simply by laying one of her hands on him, hands she herself calls rough and sweet—and, I would add, wise? I once knew a shepherd from Abruzzo, a shepherd of sheep rather than souls. He had survived the death throes of the *transumanza*, the process of taking livestock into the mountains each summer. He outlived the death of one civilization, of goats and sheep, to see that of another, of supermarkets and cans of tuna. He told me that one day he became aware that he had a special power in his hands, which were always warm and welcoming. Once when he fell and hurt his knee, he cupped his hands on his kneecap. After a few minutes of concentration, he was no longer in any pain. And another time, when a sheep was caught in a trap meant for wolves and broke its leg, he held that broken leg tightly in his hands for a good hour. The sheep was healed. A miracle, perhaps? From that moment on, the shepherd began to lay his hands on whoever asked him to, and lately it's occurred to him that he should make people pay him. He rested his hands on my back when it ached, and I have to say that I felt better. The placebo effect? An illusion? I don't know. Our bodies certainly possess powers of which we're unaware, and that we clearly underestimate.

But if Clare had these powers in her hands, then why didn't she cure her own legs—those legs that refused to carry her even from one room to another? Why couldn't or wouldn't she leave behind an illness that gradually killed her after she had spent twenty-eight years in bed? Am I crazy to say that Clare's illness was a sign? A language that spoke in lieu of a mute tongue?

Dear Author,
They don't know what kind of ailment Clare suffered from. Not a single biographer, historian, or writer says why. Nobody knows. I asked a doctor and he told me that there are a number of possibilities. It could have been rheumatoid arthritis. But no one ever described Clare's symptoms.

Dear Chiara,
Did you know that my sister died of rheumatoid arthritis, which tormented her for many years? I recall that first she found lithium to be helpful. And then cortisone, which made her swell up. And when cortisone no longer worked, she began losing weight. She became like a little bird, her thin shoulders sticking out from behind. And then came the collateral damage: heart disease, an occlusion in her throat that made them cut a hole in her neck so she could breathe through a narrow tube covered by a gauze pad. She died young, in a hospital in Rieti, and I can't forget those final days of her suffering and unraveling.

Dear Author,
I know, because you wrote about her in a little book that I devoured with my typical enthusiasm. I was struck by your description of your voyage into the subterranean depths of the hospital, guided by a Charon-like figure with latex

gloves and a limp. And the sight of that comb abandoned on a cart that you didn't recognize. Grief can take mysterious paths, sometimes even grotesque ones. But why did Clare get sick? Do you think that there is always some reason why we become ill? Or is it about familial destiny, and that's it?

Dear Chiara,
If only I knew! My partner, the actor and musician Giuseppe Moretti, died a young man, the same exact age as his father when he passed away. He left us on New Year's Day, his hand in mine. He was breathing erratically, as if to suck in the air that he lacked. When he stopped gasping for that last slender thread of air and his chest became still, his mother Caterina said, "He's finally asleep." But instead he had died. Poor Caterina! She had so longed for a son, whom she loved beyond every human law.

Dear Author,
Let me steer you back to Clare of Assisi. Before that sickness we know nothing about, she had been a young girl full of energy, enterprising and determined.

In the *Legend* or *Life of Clare*, one finds this: "On Palm Sunday, the blessed child dressed and respectfully adorned herself and went to the church with the other women to hear Mass and receive the palm from the bishop. And so, things happened in this fashion: all the people were there to receive their palms from the bishop, but she alone did not move, she alone did not go with her friends to receive her palm. When the bishop saw her standing withdrawn and alone as though she was ashamed, God inspired him to descend from his chair, and paternally he went over to give her the palm, and he blessed it."

Isn't this the portrait of a willful adolescent? When all the young girls went off to receive their palm and have it blessed by the bishop, she held herself back, taciturn and quiet, as though she were waiting for someone. The bishop realizes this and rather than calling her to him, he goes over to her. Seeing her ashamed and alone, he gives her the palm and blesses it. What does that mean? That Clare didn't want to get mixed up in the crowd? That she was proud and aloof? Or that she was tired of the songs she had heard, tired of the atmosphere of a church that felt to her like her future home, preferring to be still so she could hear the voice of God calling her to him? Some maintain that everything had been arranged in advance, that Francis had worked things out with Clare and the bishop Guido, who was his friend, so as to make public his fondness for this little lamb, so pious and devoted.

Dear Chiara,

I'm in the midst of reading the collection of testimonies for Clare's canonization process. It's been edited with particular care, even affection, by Father Giovanni Boccali and published by Porziuncola Press. The original is in Latin and has unfortunately been lost, it seems. We have access only to a sixteenth-century transcription, translated by one Sister Battista Alfani from the convent of Santa Maria di Monteluce outside the gate of Perugia. The style of Sister Battista is fluent and clear but also attentive and never careless. It's a rigorous style that follows the argument, respects each witness, seeks to smooth out one's reading without adding anything extra of its own. It's been a pleasure to read. "The following night, as she had already arranged with St. Francis, she chose a companion she trusted. She didn't want to leave through the main door of her house, for she didn't want to be heard or stopped." And so we have the description of Clare's escape. It's not just any escape. The girl leaves silently, in the middle of the night—maybe carrying her tiny shoes made of deerskin that fit her so well. It seems that Francis had told her to arrive dressed as usual, stuffed into her brocade and silk. She left her room on tiptoe so no one would hear her. She approached the little door, the side one that was always closed, to be opened only if a corpse had to be removed. The dead cannot go out through the main door by which one leaves but also re-enters. Her departure had to have something definitive about it, expressing her final goodbye to her home.

From that door symbolizing the body's farewell, Clare goes out into the street. The legend tells us that the door was sealed with stones and bars, in such a way that a young girl would have had difficulty opening it. Yet Clare succeeds. Was it with the help of Christ? Or had Saint Francis thought of something? The fact remains that she opens this sturdy little door dedicated to the dead and heads out into the darkness of the sleeping town.

To arrive at San Damiano, she had to travel some distance on foot. Five kilometers, writes Giovanni Boccali. Would she have carried a lantern? Was there a full moon to illuminate her path? Was she wearing a mantle that covered her head? What would she have taken with her, the young Clare? Nothing, says the legend. She left everything she owned at home. Perhaps even her shoes.

But where is the barefoot girl going, daughter of Favarone Scifi di Offreduccio and Madonna Ortolana Fiumi? To the monastery of Santa Maria of the Angels, called the Porziuncola. Where Francis is waiting for her, with his companions in prayer. It's not hard to imagine the little church, the handful of brothers—barefoot as well?—praying out loud in the midst of a circle lit by candles. They were stumps more than candles, made from a cheap wax that sent out a strong odor of sawdust.

Actually, it wasn't even beeswax, but the fat of oxen. And it unleashed a gray, oily smoke that stank and scratched one's throat.

Clare arrives. Will they have heard the faint sound of her unshod feet on the stone pavement? Would they have heard the dog barking in the courtyard of the monastery? Or did they notice the flames of the candles flickering when the main gate was opened? The brothers greet her affectionately. We'll never know if they embraced her. A chaste, brotherly embrace, but welcoming. It was forbidden to the friars to embrace a woman, even one ready for consecration. It is likely that they formed a circle around her and that the circle was broken to give space to Francis. But had Clare and Francis planned her escape ahead of time?

Dear Author,
Yes, it certainly seems that Francis and Clare had spoken, but it's not known when or where. It wasn't easy for a girl from a noble family to go out by herself or to meet up with a man, even if he was a friar. Especially a man who'd become a friar only recently, and who hadn't yet taken holy orders. Francis was known throughout Assisi as Pietro di Bernardone's crazy son who stripped himself naked in front of everyone, leaving his clothes and all his belongings to his father and then holing himself up with some friends in an abandoned church. He went about town barefoot, wearing a tunic made of rough wool outfitted with a hood, carrying around with him neither silver coins nor rings but only a cord that he wound around his waist and a walking stick.

Dear Chiara,
What could have moved Francis to convince Clare that she should follow his example of poverty and renunciation? Did

he feel affection, tenderness, curiosity for this judicious and intelligent child? Or was it political calculation that led him to involve one of the wealthiest and most beautiful girls of the city in his mad project of denial and renunciation? Clare's response, however, went well beyond mere political or emotional consent. Hers was a vocation; I can find no other word to explain a choice so radical and definitive. A choice from which Clare never veered and one which she never repented. Perhaps her body had wanted to say something profound—but it was silenced. A body that reacted instead with a silent and devastating illness.

Dear Author,
So now you've already entered into the story. You've already grasped the thin little hand of Lady Clare, daughter of Favarone di Offreduccio and Ortolana Fiumi. You decide how to continue. I wish you a good journey. At the end of your voyage, I'll ask only that you vouch for me. Once I know who my namesake really was, I'll better understand myself and my destiny and, I hope, something about why I'm in the world, which is an enigma to me. I'd like to figure out how to stop fasting, but that will happen only if I can manage to possess a happy body. You set forth the hypothesis that Clare's body wasn't a happy one, notwithstanding the extreme joy she knew from spiritual ecstasy. Where do you get this from—the fact that she was sick? And what if her illness was even a way of affirming an iron will, of subjecting her body to her spirit?

Dear Chiara,
Certainly, in today's eyes, this relentless obstinacy of an iron will pitted against a young woman's body seems like utter madness—so determined was she to seek out mortification

and sacrifice. But how much of this stubborn humiliation of the body belonged to her epoch, and how much to her, that willful and determined girl? Didn't the Church consider the body an enemy to hold at bay, and in the event of violent temptations, to torture and constrain? "The devil is the inventor, the patron, and the profiteer of dance and all its forms": that's what I read in a book by Eileen Power, *Life in the Middle Ages*, where she paints a fetching portrait of one Madame Eglantyne, a young girl from a good family who becomes the vain and careless abbess of a convent in the north of England. Even words were considered dangerous expressions of the body. One's voice should leave one's mouth only in prayer. Any other discourse was considered useless and harmful. That's why nuns often utilized the alphabet of sign language to communicate among themselves.

That's what Clare does at San Damiano when she discovers that one of the nuns has stayed in bed rather than going down for the morning prayer—the hardest prayer, because it meant getting up out of bed at two in the morning. She goes to look for her in her room, she touches her shoulder and then signals to her that she should come down at once because she's late. And the nun obeys, rubbing her eyes. We can imagine these girls clothed in their long white robes, their hair cropped short. Certainly they wouldn't be wearing their veils while they slept. How often were they able to wash their hair? Would some of them have had lice? Clare, whom Francis made an abbess against her will, had to think about this kind of thing as well. I imagine her as she runs to prepare a potion consisting of pitch and oil to kill the parasites she found on the head of a novice who was scratching herself all day long. Lice back then were extremely common. I remember reading one of Tolstoy's letters—and we're talking about six centuries later—in which he writes about what would happen when a new guest would come to stay in his villa in the countryside. They would send a servant to sleep in his bed the night before he arrived, so the fleas would all crawl onto the servant's skin, and the visitor would subsequently be left unscathed.

In a document cited by Eileen Power that draws on the letters of a Parisian householder from the fourteenth century—a *ménagier*—to his wife, I found this regarding fleas: "In summer take heed that there be no fleas in your chamber nor in your bed, which you may do in six ways, as I have heard tell. For I have heard from several persons that if the room be scattered with alder leaves the fleas will get caught therein. Item, I have heard tell that if you have at night one or two trenchers of bread covered with birdlime or turpentine and put about the room with a lighted candle set in the midst of each trencher, they will come and get stuck thereto. Another way which I have found and which is true: take a rough cloth and spread it about your room and over your bed and all the fleas that may hop on to it will be caught so that you can carry them out with the cloth wheresoever you will. Item, sheepskins. Item, I have seen blankets placed on the straw and on the bed and when the black fleas jumped upon them they were the sooner found and killed upon the white. But the best way is to guard oneself against those which are within the coverlets and furs and the stuff of the dresses wherewith one is covered. For know that I have tried this, and when the coverlets, furs, or dresses in which there be fleas are folded and shut tightly up, in a chest bound with straps or in a bag well tied up and pressed, or otherwise compressed so that the said fleas are without light and air and kept imprisoned, then they will perish and die at once."

Surely there were no furs in San Damiano, but there were covers of coarse cloth, and perhaps even some sheepskins. And certainly there were fleas, as there were everywhere else.

And stinkbugs too. When she noted that one of the girls was continuously scratching her head, Clare had to run to help her, otherwise those lice would spread throughout the entire convent. But where to find alder leaves? Assisi's housewives used pitch and oil or vinegar against lice. But what to do in a house where all was held in common at Clare's insistence, deprived of everything? Even water was rationed. How to wash off your dirty feet after a day of running about on dusty floors and through the muddy cloister? Hot water was available only when there was enough wood to light a fire. If Friar Leo or Friar Jacob hadn't arrived with an armload of wood, you couldn't even heat up the tiny portion of chickpeas a kind peasant had left for you, dug out of a sack now practically empty.

This was why Clare fought against enclosure. It deprived the nuns of the liberty of moving about in search of food, or alms, or work to sustain themselves. Francis had taught that whoever places himself in God's hands must do so sincerely and absolutely, without holding back. To survive you could perform manual labor—in exchange for which you asked not for money, but for food—or you could beg. One shouldn't feel ashamed asking for a piece of bread. And even if you did feel a bit of shame when you begged, that was good: it meant that you were mortifying your pride, humbling an "I" that was too human and egocentric, an "I" in constant need of correction.

There certainly wasn't much time to think about oneself or one's own body when you needed to follow the rules of the convent. The sisters had to get up at six to recite the First Prayer (Prima), after which they could make a light breakfast for themselves with water and bread. Then there were all the chores to do in order to run the convent and keep it clean: cooking food for about twenty sisters, making up the sacks of straw and getting rid of dust and insects, working in the orchard, washing the laundry and hanging it out to dry in the sun, sifting the flour or cleaning the lettuce that one of the two brothers assigned to farm work had gathered for them, drawing water from the well, taking care of nuns who were sick. The prayers of Terce followed, and then those of Sesta and Nona, after a sparse dinner of greens and some bread, if there was any, or a bit of cheese. Then Vespers and Compline, recited at seven in the evening. They went to bed only to wake up at two, descend into the cold, dark church in bare feet to recite matins (Mattutino). The nuns could then go back to bed, but only for three hours, after which they had to get up again to greet a day full of fasting and prayer and domestic chores. Clare was the first to rise, the last to lie down, always ready to fast and pray.

"And certainly she was most diligent with respect to exhorting and watching over her sisters, and she had compassion on those who were ill. And she was solicitous when it came to serving them, meekly submitting herself even to the most servile tasks, always humbling herself." So says Suor (Sister) Cecilia, "daughter of Master Gualtieri Cacciaguerra da Spello, a nun from the convent of Saint Damiano," at the hearing for Clare's canonization, which took place between October and November of 1253, barely three months after the saint's death.

We can imagine our Clare, with her calloused feet and hands ruined by domestic work, never losing her calm even when faced by the difficulties of caring for the sick, whom she tended to indulge: "Humbly submitting and abasing herself." But why such scorn? Was it an exercise in self-punishment? Or did Clare really despise herself? Did she consider her young body still too demanding despite its mortifications, too alive and curious about the world?

Suor Cecilia adds this: "She was never upset, Madonna Clare, but with much sweetness and benevolence would teach the other nuns. And sometimes, if necessary, she would diligently reprimand them." It couldn't have been easy to deal with those extremely young novices, some of them sent by Francis himself. He was so terribly convincing when he spoke in public that young girls ran to ask his advice, and he would invite them to join Madonna Clare in the convent of San Damiano.

How many arrived in the grip of feverish enthusiasm! But then once they realized all the sacrifices they had to make— lives spent in hunger and never enough sleep—how many went on to lose heart, becoming churlish, angry, defensive? Such things happened. But Clare knew how to convince them. Not with authority and force but through example and her untiring, generous availability. As Suor Cecilia says in the canonization records, Clare "would wash off with her own hands the backsides of the sisters who were sick, which were sometimes infested with worms."

A crude image that helps us understand what life was like in a convent of women sworn to absolute poverty. It's likely that Sister Cecilia was talking about a few elderly nuns who were incontinent, who would defecate while sitting in their chairs. And who knows? Left abandoned to themselves for hours at a time, maybe they didn't realize that right beneath them worms were festering. At this point, someone alerted by the stench would warn Clare, or perhaps she herself realized that no one had cleaned these poor, elderly women and she would arrive to do it herself. With the sparse amount of water they had at their disposal—very little during the summer months when the level in the well was at its lowest— Mother Clare rolled up her sleeves and prepared herself to clean the backsides of her ill sisters, to wash off their chairs and bury the worms under the dirt of the cloister. Given her gentleness of spirit, she would not kill even the worms, because they too are God's creatures.

But as though that weren't enough, Suor Cecilia adds, "And so this very lady herself would say that she noticed nothing fetid, but almost immediately she would smell a sweet odor." This is something that struck me when reading the letters of Saint Catherine of Siena. The beloved of Christ did not chase away strong smells; she sought them out. She wanted pus, infected wounds, worms—secure in the knowledge that through the grace of Christ, she would be inhaling the perfume of violets and fresh fruit. Saint Catherine goes so far as to drink the water with which someone had cleaned the body of a leper. She does so with pleasure, even as her mouth is disfigured in a grimace of horror, even though her tongue is seized by the desire to spit it out, and her throat almost gags and chokes, refusing to swallow that putrid water. But the sacrifice prompts a metamorphosis, quickly transforming the stench into a perfume. Such is the "grace" of the Lord.

Dear Author,

By now you know more than I. I'm delighted that Clare has grasped you by the hand and is now dragging you to her side. I'm the one who's rudderless. My head is as light as a dried nut. My mouth feels drowsy, my tongue swollen. My dream of a happy body is in retreat, rather than moving forward. I feel weightless, a stray feather that could be snatched up by the next wind. I'd like to stop dreaming. But perhaps I won't, perhaps I'll take up fasting again so I can slough off my body and leave it on the bed, like a caterpillar eager to be transformed, eager to extract his crumpled wings and laboriously take flight.

FEBRUARY 13. I haven't received any more letters from Chiara Mandalà in weeks. I'm in rough waters, with a character

leading me by the hand, as she says, and I have no idea what to do with her. I've tried reaching Chiara through email, but there's no response. It's as if I'd been conversing with a ghost. Strange, strange Chiara, why aren't you answering? I've looked on the map of Sicily for Santo Pellegrino and there is no such town on the slopes of Mount Etna. Maybe there's no such girl as Chiara Mandalà either. So, with whom have I been corresponding over the last two months while books about Clare of Assisi were piling up on my desk? She briefly interrupted her silence when she asked for a list of the books I'd been collecting, and she registered me on some system that allows computers to exchange information without going through email—something I had no idea you could do. Since then I haven't had another word from her. It looks as though I have to go on alone. I'll try to keep a journal; maybe that will help. I miss my interlocutor, my desperate Sicilian. But I'll have to make a virtue of necessity and learn how to converse with myself.

FEBRUARY 14. I'm looking over the list of books on Clare again—the one sent off to that Sicilian girl who has so mysteriously vanished. I've found lots of others as well; some I've bought, others I checked out of the library. There's *Saint Clare of Assisi on Trial: A Spiritual and Historical Reading of the Acts of Her Canonization*—the most useful with respect to contemporary references to Clare—and *Clare of Assisi: A Silence That Cries Out* by Chiara Giovanni Cremaschi. Then another of Chiara Frugoni's books, my favorite: *A History of Clare and Francis*. There's Mary Laven's *Virgins of Venice: Broken Vows and Cloistered Lives in the Renaissance Convent*, and works by Georges Duby, Franco Cardini, Jacques Le Goff, and many others.

But the most valuable book is the one containing the testimonials by the nuns of San Damiano for Clare's canonization. These are the words of the women who knew Clare, who lived with her for forty years. And even if they wanted to favorably impress the judge who was interrogating them, their stories are essential for knowing about life in the convent. I also came across an interesting book that references a "Life of Saint Clare"—written in Umbrian dialect in the nineteenth century, and based on the *Legenda S. Clarae Virginis* of 1255 attributed to Thomas of Celano, first biographer of Francis: "And so that the dust of worldly delights would not debase or burn the heart of Saint Clare in any way, and that it would not be tainted by mundane behaviors or deeds, Saint Francis tried to devise a way to free her from this world of shadows and make her a nun."

This reference supports those who maintain that Francis had the idea that Clare should become a nun before Clare did. How, the author asks himself, could a girl of eighteen have developed a plan so decisive? How could she be so self-possessed as to abandon her home, her needlework, her parents, everything she loved, to enclose herself in the most wretched of convents, living only on alms? For those who doubt from sheer principle that women are capable of making their own decisions, the intervention of men is essential. Don't women always have to be persuaded, cajoled, convinced, almost always by stimulating their love or their envy, to the point of being browbeaten into agreeing?

The historian Chiara Frugoni suggests in her sure, scholarly tone that in wanting to reinforce his radical choice, Francis needed to bring a girl from a noble family known throughout Assisi into the mix—someone like Clare, daughter of Favarone di Offreduccio. To counter the hostility, the raucous laughter, the violence that Francis and his friends provoked as they went about barefoot in their tattered clothes, they needed smart, normal people to take part in their mission. It was as though he was saying: look, even noble families harbor the very ideas that I consider just. And who better to make this case than a rich, beautiful, aristocratic girl on the verge of a prosperous marriage: who better than she to give witness to such a thing?

All in all, it would have been a calculated move—or better, a political strategy—on Francis's part to entice the young Clare to follow in his footsteps. And as for Clare? Would such a young woman be able to fall so in love with an idea to the point that she would sacrifice everything she had, including her future? Given Francis's extraordinary intuition, it's understandable why he set out to uncover a hidden talent, a calling serious and faithful to itself. It seems that this lovely girl from a good family may have already hatched the idea of sacrificing herself long before she met Francis. But he was smart to identify her, bring her out of her shell, confront her with her responsibilities, infect her with his enthusiasm and his passion. All of which takes nothing away from the profundity and originality of Clare's vocation.

FEBRUARY 16. A question that just hit me: Where did that ferocious desire for poverty and silence, for isolation and prayer, come from? Did it belong only to Francis and his friars, or was it circulating throughout all of Europe at the time? Didn't the urgent need to renew the Church and return to the letter of the Gospels, the disgust over the consolidation of power in the hands of a corrupt clergy, unite the most sensitive of Christians, whether rich or poor? What role did those religious and cultural movements born a few centuries earlier, such as the Albigensians or the Cathars, play in all of this?

Years ago, my sister Toni studied and wrote about the Cathars. She would talk to me about them with such enthusiasm that I got infected too and set out to read about their adventures. What moved me was the determination and dignity with which this group of men and women alike defended the purity of their faith. They embraced poverty as an achievement and a life practice, valued friendship and solidarity, rejected war, violence, and even sexual pleasure, all for the purpose of imitating Christ.

The Church had no patience for them. It immediately considered them dangerous enemies who were out to undermine its pyramidal structure of authority because they questioned the principle of obedience and refused to recognize the pope. For these so-called heretics, all were naked and equal before a God who was both loving and strict. But this was intolerable for a totalitarian vision that tended to consider the entire world its empire and living space. It was precisely to exterminate the Cathars' heresy—which spread with extraordinary speed—that Pope Gregory IX came up with the Inquisition. And he sent his armies to combat and destroy the cities that housed "those possessed by the devil." It took seventy years, but the Church got what it wanted. The Cathars were forced into exile; they were hung, quartered, and burned alive. Among the many massacres, I might just mention the one at Béziers, where 20,000 people were killed. That's the number reported by the papal legates. But the pontifical soldiers, men passionate about the crusades, boasted when they returned home of having slaughtered "at least a million people" in their furious defense of the "true faith."

The story of Montségur, the last refuge of the Cathars, is a moving one. Besieged by the papal army in 1243, it was definitively conquered and destroyed in 1244, with the massacre of all its refugees—women and children included. A massacre that remained for a long time in the memory of those walls, now in ruins. The Cathars called themselves "good men and good Christians." They didn't consider themselves heretics; they thought they were closer to Christ than the Catholic Church, a church "corrupted" by possessions, money, and business. The accusation stung, and the Church unleashed itself on them like a starving vulture after denigrating them, isolating them, and making fools of them.

The Church accused them of refusing the Eucharist. They accused them of not believing in Christ's resurrection, of practicing poverty, of holding all things in common, including women—which was not true—of being arrogant and insolent, of despising the Church and its ceremonies, of spitting on the host and rejecting the pope. In reality, what the Cathars preached was strict adherence to the letter of the Gospels, taking Christ's side against any concentration of power—and especially against the idea of a religious state. Purity meant renouncing all possessions, assisting the sick, helping the poor. They didn't believe that wealth made for better people but considered it a tool of the devil. Women were thought of as men's equals as preachers and in their relationships with God. That's why the Cathars were teeming with women who had turned their backs on marriage and childbearing. They could enjoy the liberty of thought and the spoken word that the Cathars' version of Christianity guaranteed to all.

The paradox is this: Inspired by the Cathars and their ideas about poverty, humility, charity, and chastity, Dominic of Guzmán founded the Dominican Order—the very order whose members became the cruelest of inquisitors. They practiced torture in the name of a cruel, intransigent God, sending to the pyre whoever strayed from paths laid out by a Church that believed itself unique in its pursuit of justice. The Dominicans deny that Saint Dominic participated in the Inquisition, pointing out that the saint died in 1221, twelve years before Pope Gregory IX appointed several Dominican friars as judges for the Inquisition's first tribunal. But there's a painting that attests to the contrary: a canvas by Pedro Berruguete called *Saint Dominic Presides over a Tribunal of the Inquisition*. The Dominicans themselves seem to have commissioned it, although it's not clear whether it was because they were trying to look holier than God by proposing that their founder was the first to pursue heretics, or because they wanted to make the severe fathers of the Inquisition look better. In any case, the painting is from the fifteenth century, and it's not known if it represents an actual fact, or a legend someone wished were true.

But it is the case that Saint Dominic came to know the Cathars when he went to preach in France, and that he was fascinated by them. After he returned to Rome, Pope Innocent III, who had become preoccupied by the spread of heresy, sent Dominic out again among the presumed heretics to coax them back into the fold. By 1203, the anti-Albigensian politics of the papacy had thus already begun; Dominic was a missionary in Languedoc by 1206.

Records tell of a Dominic torn between his sympathy for the Cathars and his obedience to the pope's repressive politics. He believed in dialogue: in convincing rather than constraining. Above all, he wanted to project an example of a faith lived in poverty and sincerity.

Similar sentiments tore Francis and Clare of Assisi apart, both of them fascinated by the idea of the church's spiritual renewal and, at the same time, bound by sincere vows of fidelity and obedience to papal authority. They were intrigued by the proposal for radical poverty but simultaneously preoccupied by the divisions within a Church they wanted to see gloriously unified. These were difficult contradictions to resolve. But miracles were possible in those restless, feverish times.

And then a miracle happened, albeit a partial one. Both Francis and Clare succeeded in getting themselves accepted by the official church while remaining faithful to the Gospels, dedicating themselves to lives of chastity and poverty, and rejecting a hierarchical and dogmatic form of politics. The Church rewarded them, or perhaps got them out of the way, by making them saints. The old Latin phrase *promoveatur ut amoveatur* is relevant here: they were kicked upstairs so they'd be quiet. But as soon as they died, the Church had its hands all over their wills and testaments, softening the rigor of the rules they wrote for their orders, and doing everything possible to restore things to business as usual. In effect, it took only a few years to whittle down their radical tendencies so they would fit within the norm—the result of the Church's insatiable, intelligent capacity, at once cynical and farsighted, to turn everything to its own advantage.

MARCH 10. I wonder if Clare read. If she knew Chrétien de Troye's *Parsifal*, a book that awakened the fantasies of the youth of her day. The story's hero adores his mother, but he loves adventure even more. He abandons his parent—who dies of grief—to wander all over the world in search of the Holy Grail, the chalice Christ drank from at the Last Supper and into which his blood was collected when he was on the cross. After becoming a knight of the court of King Arthur, Parsifal discovers the Grail in the castle of the Fisher King, but then loses it from sight. And from that moment on, every faithful Christian knight made it his duty to search for the Holy Grail, which over time became ever more mystical and abstract.

Ortolana, Clare's mother, came from the venerable family of the Fiumi. She received a good education, the kind given to girls of a marriageable age from rich and noble families with international ties. She had enough musical training to be able to entertain the family, sufficient learning to read at least those few books written in the "langue d'oc" and "langue d'oil"—Occitan and French—that young girls of marrying age were allowed to read, and a smattering of classical culture so as to hold her own in conversations of substance. Would Ortolana have read the *Lais* of Marie de France, which weave together the real and the marvelous? Would she have dreamed about the story of the man who is changed into a wolf, or a fairy who lusts after a human? Who's to say that she wouldn't have known the entire cycle of stories about King Arthur's knights, Queen Guinevere's clandestine love affair, the wizard Merlin, Tristan and Iseult? She might have laid her eyes on the *Song of Roland*, with its tales of the good Orlando and the traitor Ganelon. When I was a teenager, I used to go to warehouses in Palermo to watch puppets fighting on stage with their marvelous rhythms of jumps and turns and the pattering of feet on wooden boards as they brought their duels to a close. The Knights of the Round Table from the Carolingian cycle were moral men attached to principles of loyalty, courage, generosity, compassion for the weak and infirm, fidelity, and religion.

Ortolana was a cultured and independent woman. While her husband was engaged in faraway wars and crusades, she went to Rome to visit the tombs of the apostles. Thereafter, in the company of Pacifica di Guelfuccio, she decided to travel all the way to the Holy Land, wanting to go in person to visit the grotto in Bethlehem where baby Jesus had been warmed by the breath of a donkey and a cow. These weren't easy trips. Nor were they without their share of dangers for two young women born and raised in a small town like Assisi in the first decades of the thirteenth century. But contrary to what we might think, this was a period of tireless travelers. And they traveled especially to holy sites, refusing to be discouraged by difficulties of any kind: poorly maintained streets, broken-down carriages that could barely move, bandits from whom they were lucky to escape with their lives if not their possessions, the scarcity of decent lodgings and having to sleep in barns on top of hay alongside donkeys and oxen, miles of travel on foot, thin pickings for food—none of it ever good—and the imminent threat of disease. All this notwithstanding, people were constantly going on pilgrimages. So many culinary practices, languages, fashions, tastes, and stories traveled from one part of Europe to another along with those intrepid pilgrims.

MARCH 25. Nights of insomnia. The yearning for sleep weighs down my eyelids, and they grow heavier and heavier. But I barely close my eyes only to open them immediately, in a panic—as though I'm going to hurt myself by going to sleep, as though I'll be kidnapped and carried off to some dangerous, far-off place. So I just force myself to keep my eyes open. As a distraction, I pick up a book and start reading, staying awake until the volume slips out of my hands. At this point I turn off the light. Maybe now I'm ready to sleep, I tell myself. Instead, as soon as I lie back down on the mattress, a piercing thought crosses my mind: the fear of loss, the loss of consciousness. Maybe I'm ebbing away and don't realize it. Maybe somewhere out there, beyond sleep, death lies waiting. I need to stay awake to know that I'm alive, to find myself conscious and aware. I don't want to die in the dark, unprepared. And so I turn the light back on and keep reading until I really do nod off. But it's a light sleep that is disturbed by the first faint sound.

As I'm struggling to trick sleep into taking me with it, the book sliding down my thigh, I try to imagine the young Clare as she was painted with a Byzantine touch, stylized and doll-like in some of the images reproduced in Chiara Frugoni's beautiful book, *An Inhabited Solitude*. They're miniatures from the fifteenth century in vibrant hues, now in the Landesbibliothek in Karlsruhe, Germany. She's a little prissy, this girl dressed in brightly colored clothes, her blonde hair in curls, her mouth the shape of a heart. But the fairy-tale style is also quite charming—there's something folklorish about it, like a nursery rhyme. Much more austere are the fifteenth-century paintings by Giovanni di Paolo and Meo di Guido da Siena, who show Clare standing next to Francis. His ears stick out, and his mouth is a bit crooked. His hands are holding a cross and his bare feet are marked by the stigmata. Clare's face is the shape of an oval, smooth and perfect. Her eyes are wide, almost oriental, her small mouth firm and decisive. Those lips suggest ferocious tenacity—just what she needed to follow the decision she's made and to which she'll remain faithful until death, without ever getting discouraged or losing heart.

But is it true that Clare never lost heart? She would have been inhuman if she hadn't had doubts and uncertainties, like anyone else. She dedicated herself to a life of backbreaking poverty. Sleepless nights, shoeless feet on stones that were freezing in winter and scorching in summer, clothes made of coarse wool, hunger on days when nothing arrived at the convent to eat—not to mention all the days when she fasted. With very little water for washing herself, prey to the most basic diseases: erysipelas (skin rashes), scabies, bronchitis, typhoid fever, pustules, malaria, worms.

If you were a little knowledgeable about medicine, you turned to Galen or Hippocrates and their theories on fluids: black bile, yellow bile, phlegm and blood, liquids produced by the body's various organs. Good health consisted in balancing these elements, in achieving a kind of equilibrium through diet, medicine, or bloodletting by applying leeches. Would Clare have believed in Galen's explanations, which circulated in learned books of the day? Or would she have been ignorant of them? Would she have trusted the practice of bloodletting or would she have preferred medicinal herbs, their use handed down through peasant lore? Seeds of skullcap for headaches and stomachaches, lungwort for respiratory infections, aloe for inflammations, burdock for the liver, milk thistle to stave off indigestion, echinacea for coughs, ficus for maladies of the thyroid, lemon balm as a sedative?

But medicine cost money. Doctors, who often performed the work of dentists or surgeons, demanded to be paid. Money didn't circulate in the monastery of San Damiano. That's why the sisters cultivated a small garden with some medicinal plants whose leaves or flowers or roots they would boil and give to their infirm sisters to drink. Mallow, hawthorn, tarragon, valerian: there was something for all tastes, and some of the nuns knew quite a lot about these plants. Customs were handed down from mother to daughter, especially in the countryside, even if they were surely only approximate remedies, albeit applied in pragmatic fashion. This is why when the nuns were sick they preferred going to Clare and asking her to lay her hand on the place where it hurt. Usually it worked.

MARCH 28. I dreamt that Clare was singing while she tapped a bare foot on the floor of a kitchen barely illuminated by a high, dusty window. Another nun, it may have been Pacifica di Guelfuccio, one of the first women to follow Clare to San Damiano, was lighting the fire with bits of wood that she had gathered in the woods nearby. Clare's voice sounded gentle and sweet to my ear. I don't know what she was singing— perhaps a nursery rhyme. But no children were near her. Clare loved children. That's what the sisters say in their accounts for her canonization. It seems that children were allowed inside San Damiano. The peasants would bring them to Clare so she could heal them. The sisters tell of a young boy who once came to her with a pebble stuck so far up his nose that it wouldn't budge. Clare touched him and the stone slipped out in a second: "A child from the town of Spoleto named Mathiolo, three or four years old, had put a little pebble in one of his nostrils in such a way that no one could get it out and it seemed that the boy's life was in danger. When he was brought to Saint Clare, she made a sign of the cross above his head, and instantly that stone tumbled out of his nose and the little boy was freed." Sister Benvenuta of Peroscia—the medieval name for Perugia—gives this account.

In my dream Clare was singing. Strange, because the convent rule was silence. And song, unless it was a hymn to God, was prohibited. Even while I was listening to her song I was thinking that perhaps she shouldn't have been doing that. Then I realized that her mouth was closed; it wasn't Clare who was singing. But from whose mouth could that voice have emerged, given that the other nun was intent on dodging the thick smoke rising up from the wet wood, her lips pressed firmly together? This is what came to mind while I dreamt that Clare's body, absorbed in her chores, was singing. She wasn't a ventriloquist. It was as though parts of her body were singing—perhaps her hands dirtied with smoke, the nails broken and blackened, or her feet with their thick, wrinkled calluses that looked like old walls where the water has leaked through. As if they were sending forth this tender voice with a sense of relief.

Calluses do grow on bare feet. No one ever had to struggle more with poor, callused feet than Clare of Assisi. Feet that for her first eighteen years had been cushioned inside soft slippers with flashy buckles that glittered beneath her brocade dress. Feet that from one day to the next were stripped of their stockings and shoes and constrained to walk on stones, on earth, in the dust—no doubt stunned the first time they touched the rough floor of the convent. Early on, delicate and accustomed as they were to being protected, they would have gotten cut when they came down on a chipped stair or brushed against the thorns of the mulberry bush in the courtyard. Chronicles tell us that shoes were permitted only for the *servitiali*, the servants who could leave the convent and to whom were entrusted all interactions with the outside. Inside the convent, you went about without shoes.

How long would it have taken Clare's feet to get used to going around barefoot? How long would it have taken for calluses to form on her heels or under her toes, so her feet could tolerate the rough clippings that coated the flowerbeds of the cloister, or walk through the fertile, muddy soil in the garden covered with sharp stones, without tears coming to her eyes?

But Clare welcomed pain. She sought it out, she beseeched it. This is something all the sisters discuss during the canonization process: "Lady Clare, abbess of the aforementioned convent, came to the monastery when she was still a young girl, and she would wear a hair shirt made of braided horsehairs. Once this lady lent her hair shirt to this witness for three days, during which time it stung her so much that she couldn't possibly bear it": so says the young girl Agnes, who returned the shirt to Abbess Clare because she found the chafing of those plaits of horsehair on her bare skin intolerable.

So Clare not only went about shoeless and wearing a rough tunic, but she tortured herself by wearing a hair shirt on her naked skin. Or an undershirt made of boar's hide. Agnes went on to testify that "the holy Clare once had made a certain vest made from boar's skin for her, and she wore it with the hairs and the bristle against her skin. And she wore this hidden beneath her tunic of coarse wool."

Clare never said anything about how she tortured her body in private. But in a community, inside a convent with no doors, it's difficult to hide much of anything. In fact, asked how she knew about those garments of boar's hide, one of the nuns replied "that she found out from her own sister, who told her that she had seen one of them. She learned that [Clare] was very discrete about wearing it, so she wouldn't be chided by the sisters. But after the lady became sick, the nuns removed those rough garments from her body." Thus at the moment of her illness, the secret of Sister Clare's hair shirt was revealed, and it was forcibly removed. On that occasion, all the nuns saw and understood what Clare had subjected herself to: this Clare who, as they said, "never wanted to forgive her own body."

In such a close space, it was impossible for the nuns not to know everything about one another, even their most guarded secrets. For one thing, they all slept together in a large room on the second floor. Except for those nuns who were taken elsewhere when they became sick, they saw each other all the time. Clare had a particular weakness for the sick, to the extent that she exempted them from fasting. Once she even sent a warm egg to a nun who had probably fasted too much and who was languishing on her mattress. Does a warm egg mean that it had been fried? Or as I read in another medieval testimony, it may have been an egg boiled inside the shell and carried by hand to the sick woman so she could suck up its contents through a small hole made with a knife at the top.

As in any crowded community comparable to a prison, there will always be impatience, jealousy, resentment, small acts of violence to punctuate the shared lives of human beings, men and women alike. Relying on wisdom and teaching by example, Clare sought to set things right. If a nun rebelled against the rules—some were only girls and had a hard time adapting to the convent's strict practices—she knelt at their feet and admonished them in tears. One witness confirmed that "When the above-mentioned Lady Clare saw one of her sisters suffering from some temptation or tribulation, she would call her confidentially, and weeping, console her. Sometimes she would throw herself at her feet."

First and foremost, she set a good example. A person in charge should behave better than everyone else; otherwise she loses her authority. And Clare was greatly respected. If confronted by the angry outburst of a weak and sinful creature, an occasion that could compromise any show of authority, Clare was not beneath begging. Weeping and kneeling before a disobedient nun could only prompt surprise, shame, or the desire to follow in Clare's footsteps. She did not command: she implored. And she got what she wanted for the good of the community: silence, communal work, prayer, sacrifice, self-control, peaceful cohabitation. The nuns knew that she never asked for anything for herself, for her own peace or comfort or satisfaction. She sought only the tranquility and well-being of the community, and that's what made her impossible to resist.

Suor Benvenuta of Perugia claimed that "The aforementioned Mother holy Clare, before she became ill, was so abstemious that throughout all of Lent and again during the Lent of Saint Martin [between All Saints' Day and Christmas], she would eat only bread and water, except for Sundays when she would drink a little wine, when we had some." I wonder if wine was a consolation, a way of easing her mind, or if she symbolically ingested it in order to bring herself nearer to the blood of Christ: "Drink, this is my blood." Through one's blood flows one's soul, as vampires know.

But Clare drank very little—practically nothing. I think that wine helped her defend herself from that severe, internal judge who prevented her from sleeping and eating and resting, even forbidding her the pleasure of eating a piece of fresh fruit: "And three days a week, Monday, Wednesday, and Friday, she didn't eat anything at all . . . until Saint Francis instructed her to eat something every day. And so out of obedience she would take some bread and water," said Suor Benvenuta. So Francis himself had to tell her to force something down; otherwise she would have become too weak. And Clare obeyed, as she always did when it had to do with Francis. But she did so without enthusiasm. She might eat a little more, but out of a sense of duty, certainly not for pleasure. The pleasures of eating had become irksome, like the taste of confinement, like the taste of duty.

MARCH 30. The feet of the nuns of San Damiano would have gotten dirty and encrusted with mud when it rained. And Lady Clare insisted that they wash off their feet before going to sleep. But since you had to go out to the well to draw water, and since it was tiring to haul up the bucket, and since it was cold outside, many of the nuns, especially the older ones, would rub their feet off with a rag, and then hide them under the covers—although we shouldn't expect them to have had sheets; did the mother of Christ have sheets on her bed? Then Clare herself would go out into the courtyard, immerse the bucket in the well, and pull it up with the strength of her own arms. She'd pour the water into a basin and carry it into the kitchen, where she would wash her sisters' filthy feet: "Such was the humility of our blessed mother that she would gather everything by herself and place it before the other sisters, making herself the least of all, giving them water with her own hands and washing their feet, even those of the sisters who were servants": thus said Suor Philippa, daughter of Master Leonardo de Gislerio.

The nuns say that once when she was washing the feet of one of the servants of the convent, "she wanted to kiss them, but the servant withdrew her foot and in doing so struck the holy mother in the mouth with her foot. Despite such a thing, she kissed the sole of the foot of the aforementioned *serviziale*." Not only did she not chastise the servant who had so clumsily moved her foot and struck her in the mouth, but she took that foot in her hands and kissed the sole.

The nuns were quite moved by their abbess's reaction, as Sister Agnes attests with regard to another episode: "This lady was so humble that once, when she was bathing their feet, she drank the water from the basin in which those feet had been washed, and it seemed to her so sweet and delicious that she could barely describe it." How can we imagine those rough, determined little hands lifting up the basin full of dirty water and carrying it to her mouth in a slow, decisive gesture? There would probably have been ants floating in there, tiny leaves that had been stuck to the soles of their feet along with dirt. Would the nuns have watched her with surprise? This was hardly an ordinary gesture. And it clearly carried symbolic weight. How much would she have drunk of that filthy water, the young determined Clare? One sip? Two sips? And was it only to give an example of her humility, or was it her determination to punish herself that led her to drink it down in lengthy gulps? The witnesses declare that she found the water in which she had washed the nuns' feet "sweet and delicious." Would she have said this in a loud voice, or would she have barely whispered? Or, as is much more likely, given the rule of silence, would she have smiled, satisfied, in such a way that everyone saw and understood how "sweet and delicious" she found that putrid water?

The judge asks if any other nun drank from the basin, and "Sister Agnes, daughter of the deceased Master Oportulo de Bernardo of Assisi, replied no, because suddenly the holy mother Clare tossed it out so that it could no longer be drunk." So the young abbess drank the dirty water and then threw it away. Why? So that the sisters wouldn't feel that it was their duty to imitate her and drink the contaminated water? The sisters of San Damiano confirmed that Lady Clare was "humble, benign, and loving." And thus, it's quite likely that she wanted to spare her sisters the sacrifice that only she succeeded in transforming into rapture.

APRIL 25. Still no word from Chiara Mandalà. It seems as though she never existed. Maybe she invented the whole thing: the village on the slopes of Etna, her father a surveyor, her mother semiliterate, the elderly chorister who gave her voice lessons. Everything, made up? One day, I tell myself, I'll go looking for her. In the meantime, I keep reading about Saint Clare and her sisters, of her stubborn and absolute determination to embrace poverty. As Suor Pacifica says, she "loved poverty." As if to say that she didn't just choose and practice poverty, but she truly loved it, the way one loves something beautiful and delightful. Suor Pacifica goes on to say that while Pope Gregory IX "wanted to give her many things and buy possessions for the convent," Clare "would never give her consent."

But poverty isn't just a pretty word, an abstract, compelling idea. Poverty means the absence of all comforts: food, cleanliness, warm clothing, a pillow for your head, a chair so you're not always on your feet, medicine for when you're sick, a blanket, a pair of shoes. Can one really love all this? Clare's response is yes, one can. Poverty was precious because she had chosen it. It had value because she had sought it out rather than having it imposed on her. When it arrives unasked for, poverty is terrible. But taken on as a commitment, it can give one a sense of great freedom. Not having to depend on anyone, not even on one's own body, is liberating. It's paid for, of course, with filth, heat, cold, inconveniences, parasites. But such things become God's blessings if they spring from a sublime predilection, signs of one's boundless sense of vocation: "She was such a lover of poverty that she reproached the mendicants from the monastery when they brought back whole loaves of bread as alms, saying, 'Who gave you these?' She preferred to receive broken bits of bread rather than entire loaves." So said Suor Philippa, daughter of Leonardo de Ghislerio, at the trial for Clare's canonization. And Suor Philippa added forthrightly, "She could never be persuaded, neither by the pope nor by Bishop Hortensius, to accept any worldly possessions!"

But how far can one go in refusing all property? And what does the word possession even mean? Shoes: aren't they a necessary possession? Isn't clothing property, even when it's a habit shared with other nuns? A bed, one made with the shoots of vines, could you call that property? Does a simple pallet belong to Clare, if no other sister would ever lie on it?

Did Philippa have her own cot, or Balvina, or any of the others? Or in refusing to possess even a sack stuffed with twigs to sleep on, could each sister sleep on whatever straw bedding she preferred, in whatever space she preferred? Was a comb an admissible piece of property? The shard of a mirror to look into to see if one's hair was tucked properly beneath one's veil, could that be called lawful property? A glass, a utensil? What about a book? And if everything belonged to everyone and everyone forswore all possessions, even the most insignificant, what then about your own body? One's hands, arms, thoughts, dreams, emotions? Were these, too, possessions to be avoided? There are moments when you have the impression that Clare went to extremes. Objects such as chairs, spoons, bowls, lids, pans, or towels did not belong to a single person but to the entire convent and had to be divided among the sisters. The body itself must be considered God's, who decides whether to keep it healthy or make it sick. And if we move on to those elusive things such as thoughts, desires, or dreams, we discover that these, too, belong to the Lord. A person might make herself the vehicle of a thought, but she will never be its owner.

There's a fine line between logic and mystery, free will and the complete surrender of oneself. We journey balanced on a thread of logic that mustn't be forced. Surely Clare had to believe that reasoning was a form of presumption, because divine language is mysterious and shouldn't be interpreted in specious ways. Divine will must be experienced, absorbed, received with one's entire self in an act of generous surrender—an act that love alone can engender in the human heart.

APRIL 27. Last night I dreamt about her. Once again it was her. Chiara, the Sicilian, was right to predict that I would find her in my dreams just as she did. But this time she surprised me. She was dressed to the nines: her little head full of curls with a barrette of pearls in their midst, a brocade dress decorated with large red lilies against a faint pink background and sleeves of white muslin, pinched together every two or three centimeters by red ribbons teeming with pearls. Her long and elegant neck rose up swan-like from her ample bosom, adorned with a necklace of diamonds that glittered in the light of the morning sun. She wore a belt of white velvet high on her thin waist, and her full skirt was gathered up in folds, strings of pearls sewn down the sides. Her feet were encased in shoes of red satin. This was the entrance of a queen: Clare, about sixteen years old. She walked slowly, making her huge dress swoosh around her, as though to say, "Here I am, everyone—look at me!" Then I realized how many people were there to see her. An admiring crowd filled the streets.

She was the bride: celebrated, awaited, admired. Two rows of servants stood erect on one side, in charge of guarding the wedding gifts: two trunks adorned with mother of pearl; a small cabinet carved from tortoise shell with a mirror housed in a silver frame; a baby monkey in a gilded cage, its face speckled with white; an oil painting of her parents austerely facing one another; a golden basin; cups designed with figures of bronze. Clare watched the servants advance, an enigmatic smile on that pale face of hers that gave her the appearance of a stunned child. I asked myself if it really was her, Clare of Assisi, this girl overdressed for a party, a petite bride in the lap of luxury.

She didn't say a word. But prompted by a sign from her father, she offered up a smile of thanks. The saddest of smiles, and completely false. A kind of brief recitation performed out of duty, that drained all the color from her face as she visibly stiffened. Her uncle Monaldo took her by the hand and led her to the groom who waited off to one side, young, dark, and handsome. The youthful Clare graciously let herself be led, but she was tense and unhappy as though she were heading to the pyre. "Where are you going?" I called out to her, but she didn't hear me. My words were lost in the darkness. I watched her raise her hand and send me a vague sign to say that she was off, as though to signal a route from which she could not deviate for any reason.

Then as she moved away from me, I saw her suddenly tear her hand from her groom's to yank off her shoes; she tossed one of them here and the other there. She untied the belt from her waist and sent it soaring up to the sky as though it were a poisonous snake. Next it was time for her jewels. She flung those into the air as well, and they landed in a ditch alongside the street. Her brocade gown designed with red lilies came off next, and finally the jewels adorning her hair. But the thread that linked the pearls together broke, and they clattered forth on the ground, all over the stones. People scrambled to collect them; filthy children dressed in rags fought one another off in an effort to grab just a single one of those precious stones. And all this while little Clare kept walking, lightly, quickly, her feet bare, farther and farther away from her bridegroom and her family. By the time she got around to removing her white, embroidered undergarment, she could scarcely be seen: a tiny, pale image against the blinding light of a huge, ponderous, rising sun.

"Marriage is central to our story . . . it perpetuates the race and marks a major change in a woman's life," writes Paulette L'Hermite-Leclercq in Georges Duby and Michelle Perrot's *History of Women in the West*. "The Church gave marriage its modern form. . . . Marriage is a sacrament [that] differed from the other six sacraments in troubling ways. It was the only one mentioned in Jewish law. . . . [And] unlike the other sacraments, it remained tainted to some degree even though it enjoyed God's blessing. Sexual reproduction was a consequence of original sin. Marriage therefore had to be indissoluble and subject to strict conditions."

How many women preferred the convent to marriage! There were lots of rules for controlling married women, often humiliating to follow: "Physically weak and morally fragile, women in the Middle Ages were deemed to be in need of protection not only from others but also from themselves," notes Françoise Piponnier in the volume edited by Duby and Perrot. In reality, the Church sought consent to marital unions, but it also permitted marriage among children. At seven years old, a girl was already considered capable of giving her consent to marry. But oddly enough, she was granted no liberty of movement or thought in any other realm. And in any case, her freedom of consent was based on a choice already made by her parents, as Piponnier explains. A freedom that really wasn't free at all.

Considered incapable of being responsible for their own sexuality and thus their chastity, women were thought of as constantly under threat. Hence the need for rigorous control and constant guidance: "It's the husband's job to tame his wife," wrote Bishop Ivo of Chartres, "just as the soul tames the body and man tames animals. The sooner she comes under the protection of her lord and master, the better things will be." In *The Taming of the Shrew*, Shakespeare had recourse to comedy to tell how a lively and rebellious girl could be domesticated. Even if by then we're no longer in the Middle Ages, but on the verge of an era of emancipation and civil rights.

At the heart of this conflict between a concept of personhood privileged by Christ, especially with respect to women, and a conviction of inferiority and innate sinfulness was the "problem of compatibility between family and spiritual life," as Silvana Vecchio has written in her essay on "The Good Wife" in the Duby volume. And naturally the question was recast in terms of female sexuality: "Humanistic works never really tackled the problem directly or never went beyond a vague, negative prejudice and an equally vague appeal for moderation. On the other hand, religious writers such as Antonino, Cherubino, and Bernardino produced reams of analyses, distinctions, and contradistinctions on the subject. The only way to solve the daily war a woman waged between the duty of absolute obedience to her husband, who owned her body, and the duty of following the path of purification and perfection the Church proposed for her soul was to produce a detailed case by case analysis of possible situations."

The complex relationship between virginity and marriage was tied up in knots. Clerics weren't able to find a way to balance their approval of sex as the only way to preserve the species with their renunciation of sexuality itself. Female purity could only be realized if all forms of sexual activity were prohibited. But ultimately, marriage was necessary for the survival of the human race. How to reconcile such misgivings about sex even within marriage with the exhortation to produce children?

In aristocratic families, the age difference between husband and wife was one way of responding to the need to ensure a bride's virginity. Sometimes the bride was ten or even twenty years younger than her future husband. Among the lower classes, the difference in age was considerably less dramatic. A laborer, peasant, or artisan needed a healthy adult woman to work alongside him, to take care of everything in the countryside and in the house. Other than tending to young children, a wife's tasks would include working in the fields, feeding the cows and sheep, drawing water from the well, combing the wool, collecting wood and lighting the fire, cooking meals, rubbing the clothes with ashes to clean them and then washing them out in communal basins, stirring polenta, kneading and baking bread, sewing garments and gluing together strips of leather to make shoes for the children, keeping an eye on the chickens. In other words, you can say that a peasant's wife was busy day and night. For sure, all good husbands, including peasants, expected their brides to be virgins, as the Church taught. Yet if by some mischance an energetic and hardworking woman didn't turn out to be a virgin, they weren't going to make a tragedy out of it. Much more important was that she was prepared to start bringing children into the world and, at the same time, willing to slave away.

In wealthy families, however, the bride's virginity was a sine qua non. That's why they preferred extremely young girls who were practically children, inexperienced and closer to purity. The husband was thought of as a guide, a model, and a teacher in addition to being owner, lord, and master. Young girls of twelve and thirteen years old were contracted by well-off families who were simply doing what they needed to do to enhance their social and economic power, as Tolstoy observes centuries later in his trenchant social satire, *The Kreutzer Sonata*, which ends with a young wife's murder when her husband suspects her of infidelity. Such a system guaranteed a bride's integrity, but it also ensured her psychic fragility and her willingness to be educated by her husband and guide.

Is that what Clare was fleeing from?

Sometimes husbands agreed to provide some form of education for their young wives, as medievalists explain. But as Silvana Vecchio observed, such education was almost always just another form of control: "To be the custodian of one's wife meant to guard her manners and behavior, besiege her with repressive attention (to make up for her constitutional weakness and moral lightheadedness), keep her out of temptation's way, and correct any fatuous or reprehensible attitudes. Correcting one's wife was considered a sign of real love and had to be accepted gracefully." Among these "corrections," slaps on the face were customary, along with whipping, locking one's wife in a dark room with only bread and water to eat, forcing her to spend the entire night kneeling uncomfortably on sharp chickpeas.

Fidelity was encouraged for husbands as well. But this was a choice a man would make freely, as a sign of his virtue, whereas his wife's so-called choice was obligatory. Otherwise she would be subject to ostracism, corporal punishment, and often death: "All the commentators on Aristotle, from Thomas Aquinas to Albert of Saxony, from Oresme to Buridanus, recognized that female fidelity was the only way to ensure the legitimacy of progeny and that a husband's control over his wife's body was the only means of ensuring his paternity." Even with this atrocious set of rules, there were still those who thought they weren't strict enough and protested the excessive liberty women enjoyed within their families. Clerics could become apoplectic just thinking about the dangers of sexual permissiveness: "The preacher Gilbert of Tournai, who was most sensitive to the psychological implications of marriage pastorals, distinguished two types of love. The first was carnal, fed by lust and characterized by excess. It was comparable to adultery in that it produced the same disastrous consequences—lasciviousness, jealousy, madness." The other type, the true conjugal love every wife was supposed to practice, had its roots "in the primordial setting of women's creation from man's rib in order to become his mate (*socia*) rather than his servant."

Yet the stereotype of the rib, as Vecchio goes on to observe, is often utilized by pastoral literature to justify women's inferiority. In the words of the medieval moralist Jacobus de Voragine, "A wife's love is perfect . . . when she is blinded by her feelings and loses all sense of proportion and truth, when she sincerely believes that 'nobody is wiser, stronger, or handsomer than her husband,' when she is pleased by everything about him, when she finds everything he does or says right and just." That's the love demanded of the good wife. This almost comic blindness is absolutely forbidden to her husband, whose love, Jacobus insists, should be "well-tempered and measured" and never excessive. St. Jerome was of the same opinion: "If it's good not to touch a woman, then it's bad to touch her: married couples live like beasts, and the act of copulation between women and men is no different than that of beasts and animals, who are without reason."

"Women are the worst of all evils. They are serpents, a poison on which no medicine will work. Women are useful only for satisfying the lust of men." These are the words of Saint John Chrysostom, who continues: "God assigned to each sex their roles in order that the most useful and necessary qualities are assigned to man, and the insignificant and inferior ones to woman. And God made it so that the man may become worthy of honor for his eminent role, and so that the female, given her lowly offices, will never think of getting on her high horse in front of her husband."

For many Fathers of the Church, sex was an absolute evil: "How will we succeed in reining in this beast?" asks the ever-anxious Saint John Chrysostom. "What limits will we impose on it? I know of nothing else like it that's not already in hell." And Saint Augustine thundered, "The greater the pleasure, the greater the sin. Whoever loves his wife with too much passion is an adulterer!"

"A man must not cover his head, because man is the image of God, and the mirror of his glory, whereas a woman reflects the glory of man. For man did not originally spring from woman, but woman was made out of man; and man was not created for woman's sake, but woman for the sake of man; and therefore, a woman must have the sign of her authority on her head, out of regard for the angels." So says Paul, in his First Letter to the Corinthians, 11:7–10. Several centuries later, a writer thought to have been Saint Ambrose would add his own comment on this passage: "A woman therefore ought to cover her head, because she is not the likeness of God but is under subjection." Apropos of Paul's injunctions later in the letter to the Corinthians against women preaching in church—"Let women keep silence in the churches, for it is not permitted to them to speak but to be subject" (14:34)—Ambrose writes. "If [women] dare to speak in church it is a disgrace, because they are veiled in order to appear humble. Moreover, women who act like this show that they are immodest, which is a disgrace to their husbands too. For when women are insolent, their husbands receive the blame as well."

"In truth, women are a feeble race and of mediocre intelligence, undeserving of our trust," insists Epiphanius of Salamina (315–403). Epiphanius was one of the first bishops of the orthodox Catholic church during the fourth century. Famous for having fought heresy, he was particularly severe with women, as though they were to blame for spreading false beliefs. Not long after him, Saint Jerome, a Doctor of the Church, would write: "The purpose of education for young girls is so they do not find out what flutes, the lyre, or the harp are for: music must be forbidden to them. Their maid must not be pretty or well-dressed, but an elderly virago, pale, serious, and squalid, who will ensure that at night they pray and sing psalms, and during the day they pray their required offices. She should not take baths, which would wound a young girl's sense of modesty, nor must she ever see herself nude. She should be raised in the cloister under the gaze of an old woman, where she will never look a man in the face; she should not even know that the other sex exists."

Fear of the female body was so severe that any hint of the ways it differed from the bodies of men confirmed its inherent and repugnant dangers: "When a woman has her discharge of blood, her impurity will last for seven days; anyone who touches her will be unclean till evening." So says Leviticus 15:19, and continues: "Everything on which she lies or sits during her impurity will last for seven days; anyone who touches her will be unclean till evening. Whoever touches anything on which she sits must wash his clothes, bathe in water, and remains unclean till evening." Later in Leviticus, we learn that "If a man lies with a woman during her monthly period, uncovering her body, he has exposed her discharge and she has uncovered the source of her discharge; they are both to be cut off from their people" (20:18). Because, as is repeated infinite times, "Adam was led to sin by Eve, not Eve by Adam. It's therefore only just that the wife accepts as her master the one she taught to sin," writes Saint Ambrose, venerated Father of the Catholic Church.

In other words, we're not born equal. Such differences are already enshrined in the fetus, as Thomas Aquinas asserts with complete certainty: "A male fetus becomes a human being after forty days, a female after eighty days. Females are conceived from malformed seed or because of humid winds." A baby girl in her mother's womb was already considered an inferior being according to natural law and genetic destiny. And natural law, one knows, can't be changed; it determines our behavior and our desires. The Fathers of the Church were all more or less in agreement when they insisted on a system of education based on women's mental and psychic inferiority, and on the need to master and control their bodies. And we're not talking about fanatics who were listened to by only a few. They were the very founders of public morality, who inspired educators, teachers, and upstanding fathers and mothers of families—even if now and then they recognized the profound injustice of their claims.

Let me list just some of their names to give an idea as to how many of them there were, and how they were revered: Saint Jerome (347–419/420); Pope and Saint Clement (second century); Saint Ignatius of Antioch (c. 35–c. 107); Saint Justin Martyr (100–162/68); San Teofilus of Antioch (second century–183/185); Saint Peter of Alexandria (d. 311), Tertullian (155–230); Saint Ciprian of Carthage (210–258); Lactantius (260–352); Saint Eustacius of Antioch (270–337); Saint Cyrillus of Jerusalem (313 or 315–387); Saint Athanasius of Alexandria (296–373); Saint Gregory Nazarene, Doctor of the Church (329–390); Saint Gregory of Nyssa (335–394); Saint Ambrose of Milan, Doctor of the Church (339–397); Saint Augustine of Hippo, Doctor of the Church (354–430); Diodorus of Tarsus (c. 330–c. 390); Saint John Chrysostom, Doctor of the Church and patriarch of Constantinople (345–407); Saint Cyrillus of Alexandria, Doctor of the Church (370–444); Saint Leo the Great, Doctor of the Church (406–461); Dionysius the Areopagite (fifth century); Saint John Damoscene, Dotor of the Church (675–749); Boethius, philosopher and saint (475–525); Saint Gregory the Great, pope and Doctor of the Church (540–604); Duns Scotus, theologian and philosopher (810–870); Saint Bernard of

Clairvaux, Doctor of the Church (1090–1153), a convinced misogynist.

MAY 16. I dreamed of a chubby baby girl, and an enormous snake that emerged from her clothes. I stared, disconcerted. But she only smiled a knowing smile. "I spit out all the venom," she said. And she had the voice of an old man. "I'm cleansed," she declared, a word that surprised me. Why did a girl who seemed to be a creature of today use a word so old-fashioned, I asked myself? But I had no answer. "Cleansed," she repeated, "cleansed of every filth." And I realized that she was talking about sex. She was cleansed because she had spat out the venom with the serpent, and the serpent represented the sexual desire of which she had purged herself.

Once I'm fully awake, I ask myself where this furious hatred of sexuality could have come from. Why, given terrible sins such as homicide, fraud, deception, theft, racism, defamation, insults, violence against the weak—why would sex have been considered, especially for women, the most insidious, most hateful, most serious, most unforgivable of crimes? Can one assume that the fear of sexuality was promulgated only by those men who took the vow of chastity, needing to construct an aura of temptation and immorality around the female body so as to keep themselves far away from it? Or was it part of a strategy of a system of power that tends to subject half of the human race for purposes of servitude? Or rather should we consider it hatred—systematically bred and disseminated—of women's freedom of thought, a constant threat for those who believe themselves to be a superior species, the sole possessors of authority and truth?

It's unsettling to think that such prejudices and sexism started not with the Church Fathers, but much earlier. They have deep roots in Greek culture, which posited the inferiority of women centuries before Christ. For the Greeks, that inferiority originated not with women falling prey to demonic temptation and their responsibility for man's subsequent exile from earthly paradise, but in an imperfection of nature itself. Aristotle, the most frequently cited of Greek philosophers during the Roman Empire and well into the Middle Ages, conjectured that woman is an imperfect human being, "a sterile man." We listen bemused as he entertains purely arbitrary theories to assert that "Since woman does not possess sufficient natural heat, she is unable to 'cook' her menstrual liquid to the point of refinement at which it would become sperm. Thus, only man contributes material to the embryo." Or as Apollo says during the trial scene in Aeschylus's *Oresteia*, a woman's body plays no role in the process of creation. It is only a vessel made to contain the male's semen. Women's role is to conserve, not create; only the male is a complete human being.

Plato had already aggravated things when he argued that the female body derived from a degenerate form of human life: "Only men are created directly by the gods and furnished with a soul. Those who live upstanding lives return to heaven, but those who are base or evil on earth—as far as we can reasonably ascertain—are reincarnated as women." All in all, the worst possible punishment: to be turned into a woman in a second life, for the misdeeds committed in the first!

What enabled this epoch-making, feminine consciousness to assert itself after so many centuries of sexist theories? Could female masochism be considered a strategy for survival? If there's no remedy against tyrants, was the only option to accommodate them, declaring your love for the bully, seducing him so as to pervert the system's internal logic? Thoroughly internalizing the idea of their own inferiority, women often become their own worst enemies, as well as other women's. In love with their fathers, they've on occasion seduced them, using the weapon of eros to reduce them to slavery, as Salome did with Herod. No other means were available.

"Chastity, humility, modesty, sobriety, silence, industriousness, compassion, care: for centuries women have heard these words repeated to them, by preachers at church, by their families, in books written just for them," says Carla Casagrande in *The Kept Woman*. "The persistence of these words in the pastoral and didactic lexicons devoted to women from the end of the 12th century until the 15th attests to the substantially long life of the model of femininity that circulated within them. . . . But a strong case for such a model was made from the very start. It was grounded in tradition, justified by Scripture, and confirmed by the providential reappearance of Aristotelian theories." It was a model responsive to the interests of not only the clergy, but the laity: "A woman who was kept at home and in the convent, whose movements, gestures, words, clothes, fertility and religiosity were kept under control, was a woman who could be led toward eternal salvation, while guaranteeing the honor and perpetuity of her family in this world—a woman approved by her spiritual directors and cherished by her father and husband."

As they faithfully carried out the will of the patriarchy, often taking out their frustrations on their own daughters, women had little occasion to foster solidarity among themselves—and then only with considerable effort. Clare succeeded in avoiding these obstacles and imposing her own will without demanding or complaining but by being cheerfully loyal to herself. It's no exaggeration to say that the determined little Clare of Assisi was a forerunner in defending women's rights, even if she never thought in terms of vindictiveness—a sentiment far from her nature and chosen way of life. But she certainly put into practice what many women wanted to do and couldn't, paying lip service to misogynistic rules while practicing her own form of liberty. A liberty that was the result not of selfishness or vengeance but of deep fidelity to her religious choices. Clare was her own mistress, free to articulate her thoughts and lay claim to a freedom that may not have had social implications—impossible in those days—but that certainly had an impact on women's thinking.

This was a legitimate form of disobedience, that of Clare and her order. They were well aware that Christ had preached the equality of all human beings—the idea that inspired Francis and Clare alike. But how could one be true to one's convictions in a world based entirely on principles of masculine domination without being branded a heretic—and treated like one? Here's where we see Francis and Clare's wisdom in action. They never sought to oppose the Church. Rather, with admirable dexterity, they tried to help the Church recover its roots, its revolutionary call to equality, its love for the other—even when the other was a woman. This was an extremely difficult task, given the tangled thicket of commonplaces, prejudices, divine certainties that the Church Fathers had gradually made into the foundation of popular culture, virtually obliterating the words of Christ. An enormous monument of a church made of expensive marble, columns, priceless altars, and sky-high roofs and terraces still overshadows and overwhelms the tiny chapel of Santa Maria della Porziuncola in Assisi where Francis first took refuge so he could preach about poverty.

MAY 26. The sayings of the Church Fathers have my mind ringing, a heavy weight. Like everyone else, I knew about their misogyny, but I hadn't known their work in any detail. I'm surprised by the words I find right in front of me, as though I were reading them for the first time. Actually, I *am* reading some of them for the first time. As I consult book after book, citing phrase after phrase, it seems that never before have I had such a clear and comprehensive understanding of what this heap of degrading assessments has meant for women—these derogatory definitions, or better, defamations, insults, suspicions, and generally malicious sentiments.

"If men could only see what's hidden beneath one's skin, the very sight of a woman would provoke vomit," wrote Odo, second abbot of Cluny. Venerated as a saint by the Catholic Church, he was one of the architects of the Clunian reform that revamped monasteries throughout the world. He started reforming monasteries in Aquitaine, in the north of France. Papal privilege entitled him to bring numerous abbeys under his supervision, and to welcome to Cluny monks from other Benedictine monasteries that had not yet been reformed. His model thus became the model for monasticism for centuries to come, one that transformed the role of religious piety into a daily way of life. These are more or less generic historical facts, but they show how important and widespread his ideas on education were.

But it was impossible to forget about the future of the species. How would the human race perpetuate itself if the body of a woman was untouchable and sex a sin that could never be pardoned? Ultimately, marriage had to be tolerated, even encouraged. Men more realistic than Odo continued to maintain that chastity was not possible for the vast majority of men, and that repression only led to prostitution, pornography, and sex outside the rules. They ended up rewriting the rules to justify this disorderly state of affairs—transforming prostitution into a practice that was regulated, validated, even romanticized. I'm reminded of Maupassant's short story "La maison Tellier." True, it's set in a different era, but it shows how the regulation of sexual disorder would persist and proliferate well into the nineteenth century, even taking on the status of myth.

Matrimony endured, however, albeit accursed: "To the woman he said, 'I shall give you great labor in childbearing; with labor you will bear children. You will desire your husband, but he will be your master'" (Genesis 3:16). All the Church Fathers and reformers are united over these words from the Bible. "Every woman must walk with Eve in grief and penance, so that with the clothing of repentance she can be fully expiated of what has come to her from Eve: the ignominy, I say, of the first sin, and the hatred inherent in her, cause of human perdition": this is Tertullian, in *De cultu feminarum* (On Female Fashion). He then adds, with complete candor: "Do you not realize that you too are Eve? God's condemnation of your sex is still enforced today: you are still to blame. You are the gateway to the Devil! You have eaten from the forbidden tree! You were the first to disobey divine law! You convinced Adam because the Demon wasn't brave enough to go after him! You destroyed man, the image of God! Because of what you did, the son of God had to die!"

Given sex's sinfulness even within marriage, the convent was considered ideal for preserving feminine virtue. But it really was a prison sentence for life, for the crime of one's genes. At the same time, women often sought out these prisons as the lesser of two evils. One didn't have to worry about sexual obligations in the convent, and in a world that characterized sex as demonic, this community dedicated to chastity enabled its members to sublimate their natural, bodily instincts through rituals, fasting, and prohibitions.

Women who chose marriage had their conjugal duties to perform, and they could expect to be pregnant almost every year—and to be faced with the real prospect of dying in childbirth, given hygienically precarious conditions. Septicemia often struck new mothers, and the number of women who died in childbirth was extremely high. In his *Daily Life in the Middle Ages*, Robert Delort observes that in the period from 1100 to 1300, there were decisively fewer women than men: "statistical studies of a large number of documents from the period proves in fact that in the 12th century, out of 200 people, 110 were men and 90 women; in the 13th century, there were 105 men to 95 women." All it took to die during childbirth was a slight act of carelessness, and the young mother could become prey to a fatal infection, leaving in her wake an infant to care for. Given the unclean hands of a midwife, dirty rags, and the lack of sterile water, it was easy for septicemia to set in. Such conditions gave rise to the phenomenon of nursemaids, peasant women from incredibly impoverished homes who for a few cents would sell their own breast milk to feed orphans. If instead a woman was fortunate to survive the dangers of childbirth, a year later she had to do it all over again and give birth to another child, and so on, year after year, until her poor body was completely worn out.

Only a few aristocratic women were able to dedicate themselves to the risky but exciting game of adultery. These women were too wealthy, too enmeshed in powerful families to be denounced or accused. Female pleasure was not considered necessary for reproduction and was thus nonexistent. It never occurred to anyone that a woman might consider such a thing important. Consequently, it was considered a grave sin. Male pleasure, indispensable for producing generative semen, was cultivated and encouraged, even at the cost of having it deviate into pornography, prostitution, and rape. All escape valves for a masculine body that considered itself the only inhabitant of a universe made in its image and likeness.

By the time she was forty, a woman had gone from being a fertile young mother to being considered a "querulous, fastidious old lady," no longer a danger to anyone. Unless she was suspected of being a witch, as could happen if she had too much acclaim as a midwife or a healer, distributing herbs and medical concoctions and sharing knowledge inherited from peasant ancestors. Medicine was too powerful and too dangerous to be entrusted to women. Besides, doctors weren't really supposed to heal the sick. Their job was to understand why God had chosen to punish one body instead of another, or why the devil used his malicious art to corrupt this soul instead of that one. Such judgments conferred power and privileges too important to renounce.

The only true goal of marriage was reproduction. Thus, anything that didn't lead to the generation of children was forbidden. Fellatio was forbidden, cunnilingus was forbidden, sodomy was forbidden. If discovered, sodomites were denounced, put on trial, and sometimes tortured and put to death. They were accused of wasting the semen of life, the gravest of crimes.

Misogyny went along with extolling virginity. The Church Fathers were obsessed with virginity, so much so that they invented the virginity of Mary for themselves. They found it inconceivable that the mother of Christ could have had sex. She must have remained a virgin her entire life, even though she had a son. Not only had she conceived as a virgin, she had given birth as a virgin. These were the awful extremes to which those theorists of purity went, even as some scholars maintain that the concept of a virgin mother takes us back to antiquity. In archaic times, before the Greeks, goddesses of war would fight alongside their sons, but they were never accompanied by adult male figures, and were thus considered virgins and mothers. But the word "virginity" had a meaning very different from that put forth by the Church. It was used to invoke the autonomy and solitude of women who chose to be mothers without the company of a man. Mary's virginity would have been superimposed onto the myth of the virgin mother and warrior of an ancient matriarchy, attested to in a few surviving statues, images carved into rock, legends handed down over the millennia.

MAY 28. Convent life has at once something monstrous and sweet about it. How does a woman voluntarily choose to remain forever inside that closed door? We know that women were forced into confinement. Alessandro Manzoni's Gertrude is a powerful reminder of this, as he describes the tragic outcome of her seclusion, unsought and detested, in *The Betrothed*. But many other women entered the convent of their own volition, like Clare. Almost as though this was the greatest thing their souls could aspire to: wall themselves in for life, cut themselves off from every relationship with the outside world, refuse to walk freely down whatever street they chose or to climb a hill to see what might be on the other side of a forest. No more admiring gazes into an expanse of water, no strolls down boulevards lined with trees, no crossing over a river on a stone bridge, no steadying a boat in the midst of waves. No exploring a far-off landscape up close, encountering other cultures and other ways of life, noticing how the colors of the stones change from one place to another, breathing in a foreign air, understanding and enabling others to understand, learning and helping others learn. These are legitimate aspirations that have been the basis for some of the most important discoveries of the world. Yet notwithstanding all that they were giving up, a number of women preferred the convent to their families. They had no alternative, unless they wanted to wait on their elderly, tyrannical fathers. Family life could be difficult, perhaps even more dangerous and cruel than the convent.

I remember visiting a Peruvian convent of cloistered nuns built in the eighteenth century. One doesn't often get the opportunity to find oneself in a convent-museum preserved just as it was 300 years ago, with its rooms, refectory, chapels, kitchens, garden, and little cells full of objects that the sisters would have used every day. I'd barely entered the dark, ample rooms covered with portraits discolored by time, when I felt a kind of distressing pang from the reaches of my memory, as though during another lifetime, I'd lived among these walls. As though I knew all the meandering corridors, redolent with the odors of rustic soup and dirty feet, having traversed them in their length and their breadth over many years. As if in some sense I had never left those narrow halls.

I remember my curiosity as I lingered in the cells, provoking the impatience of my guides. I seemed to recognize the lumps in the mattress, the shape of the pillow, the coarse blanket on that solitary cot that had rough engravings in its wood. A small, bare cell, an enormous life-size crucifix hanging from the bare, unpainted wall, the beam of the cross the color of flesh. Blood was spurting from Jesus's nailed feet, his head with its long locks of hair was bent painfully at the neck, the muscles in his arms were as thin and stretched out as cords. The only furnishings were a dark wooden bench, a kneeler, and a chest on which an old, worn-out rosary with beads of mother of pearl was nestling.

When we went down into the big kitchens where copper pans were hanging from the walls, I was overtaken by the powerful smell of chopped onions and beans boiling away in a kettle on a fire made with cinders. I could perfectly imagine the taste of the water that had been pooling for a long time inside terra-cotta jars, or the red, sour wine that would be poured frugally into the sisters' glasses. I knew how many steps you had to take to reach the basin where you'd rinse off the greens from the garden. With my eyes closed, I could have grabbed the eggs lined up on the top shelf, or the bread wrapped up in a yellow cloth. I felt under my fingers the roughness of the sand with which they would clean the plates when they'd run out of water. In the garden I recognized the extraordinary, ingenious machine they'd devised to wash their clothes. Water drawn up from the well was collected in a stone basin and drawn through a large stalk of bamboo into a wooden tub. It was then fed back into the basin by means of a clever system of leather straps. Cleansed of its soap suds, the water could be re-used.

My guides steered me toward the exit, but I resisted, because I wanted to visit every single one of the cells. I wanted to sit on the benches in the chapel and listen to the sounds of rusted bells that hadn't rung for centuries. I wanted to pause in the garden, lean over the stone well covered with an iron grate where a tall vase of geraniums now had pride of place. I wanted to open the worm-eaten cabinet where the nuns used to hang their habits. I wanted to visit the tailor shop where linen cloths were still lying in bundles. I wanted to linger over the basket of sewing equipment, to touch the white curtain embroidered in red and blue.

I watched a nun bent over her handiwork who seemed to raise her head with a hurried but sly gesture after cutting the thread with her teeth. She looked me over from head to toe as though to say, what are you doing here, don't you know we're cloistered nuns? But her eyes were sparkling, and while they looked at me with curiosity and suspicion, they invited me to get closer and watch her work. It wasn't just any old piece of needlework but an artistic composition, with an alpine landscape, featuring wisps of clouds and swallows darting around. At the top she had replaced the heads of birds with those of angels, suspended midair on fans that sprang out from where their ears should have been. When I was about to say something to the nun, she was already lost from view. Out of the corner of my eye I could make out shadows running about, and I realized that she had joined her sisters for evening prayer. In fact, the air was becoming cooler, and the sun had almost completely set. The impression of having been with them for years had excited me, but I was also exhausted.

I felt the same way when I happened to visit a convent of cloistered nuns outside Syracuse, in Sicily. As a museum it had far less to offer, but the cells had been maintained absolutely intact for two centuries. The chapel was well preserved, with simple frescoes and portraits of abbesses hanging from the walls, faded over time. In the corner of each cell you could see a wooden chest painted with meticulous care. Parrots sporting orange and blue and green feathers, flowering branches, angels flying through the woods, silver bells, butterfly-like ribbons flitting about in red and pink. Each nun had her own chest, and each chest was covered with different designs and gaudy colors, but they were all the same height and style. I asked what they were for, these boxes that were so similar and yet so varied in color and design. They told me that when the nuns first entered the convent, they would bring with them the linen and underwear from their dowries. When they died, their bodies would be enclosed within those same chests and buried in the cemetery next to the chapel. Not even in death could you leave the convent.

Yet you could write and read; in the convent you could think. In the convent there was no such thing as forced marriage or marital rape. Sex simply did not exist. The nuns would wash one body part at a time, keeping on their shirts. My mother, who attended the Sacred Heart School in Palermo when she was young, tells me that even the girls who boarded there were made to wash up while wearing their nightshirts. And we're talking about the 1920s.

What did sexuality mean for these shut-ins? How difficult would it have been for girls to repress desire until they made it disappear altogether? Did they fast and pray at all hours of the day and night just in order to suppress their senses, in all their abundance? They were certainly taught to sublimate them—graciously, joyfully, eluding the straitjackets of the censors. Sublimation has played a role throughout the history of women's experience, and it's become almost second nature. It's not to be discounted. And it might be wise to preserve this rare art of living.

JUNE 3. Yesterday, opening the door of a little shop in Pescasseroli, I saw a woman bent over her sewing, her head covered by a black cloth, and I was startled. I felt I was standing in front of a woman from Clare's order—a Poor Clare. The woman turned around and I realized she was a tailor who takes on work mending clothes. But why was her head covered? Then I remembered that she was from the Maghreb. The tenacity with which she so quickly adjusted the veil over her hair and her face when she heard the door opening left me thinking. At this very moment when women in the West are increasingly immodest about exposing their bodies, some Muslim women are becoming increasingly modest about concealing their own, until they become invisible ghosts. Does the one contrary gesture cancel out the other? Whether a woman is exposing herself beyond all limits or covering herself up against all logic, isn't it about the same thing: will-fully denying the female body its freedom?

Clare covered her head even when she was sick in bed, and she never stopped working. As one of the nuns from the canonization process said, "when Mother Clare was so sick that she couldn't get out of bed, she would raise herself up so she could sit, supporting herself with cloths tucked behind her shoulders, and she would spin. Eventually with all her sewing she produced corporals and madonnas for almost all the churches in the valley and on the slopes of Assisi." It's easy to imagine Lady Clare stretched out on the straw, her back supported by a few rolls of cloth, as she spun, sewed, and embroidered her white linen corporals. The straw was probably placed near the wall; otherwise, how would she have managed to remain seated? And what did she sew on those corporals? As we read in *Foboko*—a dictionary for writers—"According to liturgical protocols, corporals were large square kerchiefs, 60 by 60 centimeters, used for cele-brating the eucharist. Made of white cloth, of linen, they were stored in stiff bags covered with precious lining."

But what would Clare have embroidered? No one ever said. Is it likely that she sewed traditional images such as vines and clusters of grapes, the leaves of laurels and vines, roses in bloom, a golden stairway silhouetted against an azure sky? Or angels, their great wings ready to lift them up in flight? The vision of a Clare bent over her embroidery brings to mind the incredible story of Procne and Philomela, daughters of Pandion, king of Athens. When Procne's hus-band Tereus decides to marry her younger sister Philomela after Procne bears him a son, he cuts out Procne's tongue and locks her up in a prison in his castle, where she dwells in complete isolation. Only when preparations for the wedding are underway and the servants are bustling about do they permit her to lend a hand in sewing the new bridal gown. Unable to speak, Procne decides to write a message to her sister, stitching the words into a corner of the luxurious bridal gown to reveal that she's been imprisoned in the subterranean realms of the castle. Philomela thought that her sister was dead—that's what Tereus had told her. That's the only reason Philomela agreed to the wedding—even if it was her father Pandione who insisted that she wed the "poor Tereus," supposedly distraught over the death of his wife and unable to raise a young son on his own.

On her wedding day, the new bride is putting on the magnificent dress embroidered entirely by hand when she notices the writing and secretly reads it. Overwhelmed by rage, she decides then and there to kill Tereus's son in revenge. Feigning joy, she arrives at the wedding ceremony, cheerful and calm, and manages to get her husband drunk along with his powerful friends. Then she descends into the cellar, opens the door of Procne's cell, and escapes with her sister astride a pair of stolen horses. When he learns of the betrayal, Tereus follows the sisters/wives to punish them as he thinks they deserve. His is the more powerful horse, and so he catches up with them. But just as he and his warriors are about to seize them and run them through with their swords, the ruthless gods transform Procne into a nightingale, Philomela into a swallow, and Tereus into a hawk. Destined to fly, to sing, and to forever repeat the same lugubrious song.

Who knows if Clare was aware of this remarkable Greek story that recounts fraternal solidarity—solidarity among siblings? And isn't it odd that there is no word in Italian to express solidarity among sisters? There is the word *sorellanza* or sisterhood, an invention from the 1970s. And there's the forceful, utterly feminine language of sewing. Rendered mute by her husband, Procne does not give up on trying to communicate, choosing an instrument that will elicit no concern among those who control her: a needle and thread. A typical womanly activity that raises no suspicions, but rather calms and reassures. A woman who sews can't possibly sin. Her hands are too busy. She can't even write a letter; all she can do is think. And the Lord will provide some means of censuring her thoughts—the Lord who sees all and knows the kinds of things that pass through a virgin's head.

And instead, exactly where trust takes root, rebellion is born. I don't want to say that Clare had her tongue cut out like Procne. But because the convent enforced a rule of silence, her tongue lay like a dead little thing in her obedient mouth. And it's possible that Clare's busy hands told of secret dreams in that silent, visual language of embroidery. What kind of dreams? I try to imagine: Were they about her desire to fly? Her desire to see the world? Her desire to preach the word of Christ, walking like Francis beneath the sun, rather than lying there all day long on that sack of straw, embroidering corporals? I'm sure her designs were lovely. I'm sure that her hand was bold and creative. Who can really say that she didn't speak in that humble code reserved for women's fingers, while her legs lay there immobilized?

The hours would have passed slowly. And prayers weren't enough to keep her mind still. Sometimes her inert body was struck by a vision, as she dreamed with her eyes wide open. "Lady Clare recounted that once in a vision she seemed to be carrying a pot of warm water to give to St. Francis, along with a towel to dry his hands. She was climbing a steep ladder but going so easily that it seemed as though she was walking on the ground," Suor Philippa tells us. "And when she reached St. Francis, he drew out from his side a breast and he said to this virgin Clare, 'come here; receive and suck.' And after she sucked, the saint told her to do so again. And as she sucked from him, it was so sweet and delightful that in no way could she ever describe it. And after she finished, that nipple or true mouth of the breast from which the milk flowed remained between the lips of the blessed Clare, and taking into her hands what remained within her mouth, it seemed to her that it was gold, so clear and lucid it was, so that she could see herself within it, as though it were a mirror."

Clare herself recounted this dream—a dream that would have seemed like a fairy tale, given her virginal ignorance. She gathers her sisters around her to tell them of this magnificent vision. And for once, the mandate of silence is broken. The vision is simply too important not to speak of it. Clare dreams of ascending a ladder holding a pot of warm water and a towel. But the climb is so easy to her that she seems to be traveling on level ground. When she arrives at the top of the stairs, she finds Francis, who with a gentle, maternal gesture draws out from his robe a breast and extends it to his friend to suckle it. She drinks that milk which tastes so "sweet and delightful" that she can't find the words to express it. Francis orders her to drink again, and she happily holds on to his breast, and when she's finished with that divine milk she realizes that a bit of its liquid remains on her lips. Brushing it off with her fingertips, she notices that it sparkles like gold, and she sees herself as though she were looking in a glass.

A bold and wonderful dream, which would be easy, if crass, to interpret from an erotic point of view. But milk and blood were fundamental to the metaphorical language of medieval religion. Saint Catherine speaks constantly in her letters about spilling and gazing at blood; blood that courses and flows, gets collected, and loved, and drunk. She speaks of milk as the sweetest and tastiest of all food, which nourishes the spirit before the flesh.

"The good mother gives the blood of truth, the bad mother gives her breast to serpents," write Chevalier and Gheerbrant in their *Dictionary of Symbols*. "The divine mother who nurses is a sign of adoption, and thus of supreme knowledge. Heracles is nursed by Hera and Saint Bernard by the Virgin, thus becoming the adoptive brother of Christ." What is strange and unusual about this dream is that it's a man who offers milk to the virgin Clare. One might guess that for his faithful young friend, Francis was something of a mother—who nurtures her children with breast milk.

There's a great deal of sensuality as well as linguistic wisdom in this proud and personal attachment to metaphor, in a world devoid of malice and ulterior motives. Freud had not yet discovered the secret language of an unconscious eager for perverse sensualities. Back then a dream was just a dream, experienced in all its vivid colors, as though it were a drawing made by children, or a work of embroidery fashioned on rough fabric by the patient hands of an innocent nun.

In the language of signs, a virgin's milk signified immortality. Words were made up of milk and blood. Even thought itself was understood in certain cases to be permeated with milk and blood, elements with great expressive force in medieval ideas about nutrition. Milk is the first and primary food, enabling newborns to survive. I'm reminded of the dry, dangling breasts of women in some parts of Africa, thrust lovingly between the lips of babies two and three years old. Since weaning—the passage from mothers' milk to polluted water—can be dangerous, mothers nurse their little ones until not a single drop of that precious liquid remains in their dry breasts. So many young children die from drinking polluted water. And mothers know this.

JUNE 16. Was it illness that constrained Clare's movements? Witnesses said that she couldn't get out of bed. Clare went into the convent at eighteen, in 1211. According to the nuns, she first became ill in 1224, when she was thirty, and didn't leave her bed until death claimed her in 1253. Although on extraordinary occasions she would get up, supported by her sisters, and go to pray. We know of two instances when she strenuously willed herself to stand and go downstairs with the help of the robust arms of her sisters. The first time was when Assisi was invaded by the Saracens.

It was 1241; to be precise, September 9. Emperor Frederick II was locked in a struggle with the pope, who had already excommunicated him a number of times. With the help of the Saracens, he decided to invade the city of Assisi, which had sided with the pope. "When the Saracens had entered into the cloister of the said monastery, this lady let herself be led to the entrance of the refectory and had them bring her a small box containing the holy sacrament of the body of our lord Jesus Christ. And throwing herself on the ground, she lay prostrate in prayer, tearfully praying and saying these words along with others: 'Lord, protect these your servants, for I cannot.'" This is the testimony of Suor Francesca, daughter of Messer Capitaneo from Col de Mezzo. (A note informs us that Suor Francesca was the aunt of Monna Vanna, spouse of one Iacopone da Todi, who perished during a *festa da ballo* or dancing party at Pantalla, near Todi.)

Frederick's Saracens had already invaded the convent, and we can imagine the sisters' terror. This is when Clare intervenes, asking that she be carried into the refectory, where the soldiers had gathered, to throw herself onto the ground in tears. Her weeping was not so much directed to holding off the predators as it was to attracting God's attention. In fact, as Suor Francesca goes on to recount, at exactly that moment you could hear a voice "of marvelous sweetness, saying, 'I will defend you forever and for always.'" Did the Saracens also hear that marvelous voice ushering forth from the Holy Sacrament? But Clare didn't ask God to protect only the convent. "The aforementioned Madonna also prayed for Assisi, saying, 'Lord, may it please you to protect the city as well.' And the same wonderful voice magnanimously responded: 'The city will suffer many dangers, but it will be defended.'" This was why Clare was much loved and revered in Assisi, for she chased away the invaders with the power of her prayer. Historians have never been able to explain in any detail exactly what happened or what convinced Frederick's soldiers to retreat. But it's certain that they departed, leaving the city safe, and that Clare was considered responsible for the miracle.

The other time that Clare got up from her bed, if only in a dream, was on Christmas night. One of the nuns tells "how the aforementioned Madonna Clare on the night of the birth of our Lord, the one just past, was unable to leave her bed to go to chapel because of her serious illness, and so was left alone while all the sisters went to Matins as was their custom." The sisters had left her by herself, on her usual bed of vine shoots. Disappointed that she couldn't share with her sisters that moment of joy, Clare turned to heaven: "O Lord God, here I am, all alone with you in this place." On that day of rejoicing, her solitude must have felt especially harsh, but at that very instant, Clare "began to hear the organ and responsorial hymns and the entire office of the friars of the church of Saint Francis, as if she was actually there." Her stubbornly absent, immobilized body was transported as though taken up by an affectionate gust of wind, carrying her into the chapel decked out for the holy day so she could be present for the music of song and the organ, not to mention the holy offices of the Friars Minor of San Francesco.

JUNE 30. Chiara Mandalà was right: this isn't the first time I've been interested in nuns. I find imprisoned bodies of interest. I'm especially interested in the veiled body. And mutilated bodies, but also joyful ones, inhabited by a secret sensuality and open to the sublime. I'm interested in convents as places of collegiality and hidden thoughts, convents as sites of obedience—but also as spaces for a profound, mysterious freedom.

I spent three years in a boarding school in Florence, from the time I was ten until I turned thirteen. Poggio Imperiale, Santissima Annunziata: a school my parents chose so I'd be near my grandmother's house. They weren't aware—or didn't consider it important—that the school, founded in 1823 by the grand duke of Tuscany, was in a villa that was once the sumptuous court of the Medici-Lorraine princes, with frescoed rooms, gardens in the Italian style, and an enchanting view of the entire valley below. They didn't realize—or perhaps they only figured it out at the last minute—that the school "boasted," as they say in the Florentine newspapers, "a prestigious tradition at the national and international level." All just to say, I'm afraid, that the tuition was outrageous. And I had to suffer the humiliation of hearing my name called out a number of times during our communal lunches along with those of the other "defaulters." If I remember correctly, there were only three of us with parents in arrears, and thus late in paying our tuition. They threw this in our faces, not exactly blaming us, but suggesting that it showed a lack of respect for God, hoping we would feel ashamed enough to pressure our parents into hurrying up and shelling out the money.

I remember my bed being sealed off by long white curtains and the little bronze crucifix to which I prayed—in those days I was very religious and had even constructed a tiny altar to the Madonna inside my desk—and I would try to fall asleep clutching Christ's wounded body for reassurance. To be sure, sometimes in the darkness of my little room, while the others were sleeping—as far back as I can remember, insomnia has always been a part of my life—I'd ask myself what might have been the reason for such cruelty. Having recently arrived from Japan where people knelt before the figure of a corpulent young man sitting on a lotus flower, his hands clasped together in prayer, I couldn't understand this Christ with nails in his feet, a crown of thorns circling his temple, his face streaked in vermilion-colored blood. Why should a body have to suffer in order to be holy? Why did love for heaven have to take the form of sacrifice and open wounds? Back then I had no answers. My questions remained questions, and they left a bitter feeling in my throat. I would swallow hard and ready myself for sleep beneath this protective Christ whose body gave forth blood and tears.

Might these memories of confinement allow me to feel close to other secluded women from centuries ago, who certainly suffered more and had less freedom than I did? Or the bitter memories of the Japanese concentration camp for opponents of fascism—a camp where I was imprisoned along with my parents for two years when I was a child? Hunger, freezing cold, lice and fleas on my skin: these are experiences that have marked my life. I try to determine what they might still mean by comparing myself to other women who have been locked up. Is that why I feel so drawn to this subject?

JULY 2. Some time ago I had the pleasure of reading a play written by a nun around the year 1000, called *Abraham*. The author was Roswitha of Gandersheim. She lived two centuries before Clare, in a German convent, and she composed theatrical works that would be performed by the nuns. It's astonishing how much wit there is in this text, along with a delicate sense of mischief. How was a cloistered nun able to come up with the story of a friar whose young female pupil escapes from the convent and ends up as a prostitute in a whorehouse? The friar goes to find her. She thinks he's a client, and he plays along with the trick—to a point. Then at the last minute he tells her who he is and gives her a sweet, paternal sermon, reminding her that she didn't choose that profession, but that poverty and loneliness forced her into it. At the end he brings her back to the convent and everyone rejoices. How much courage she must have needed to write about this encounter between a friar and a prostitute!—and to portray a girl forced into prostitution by hunger, when everyone else would have denounced her as possessed by the demons of lust and carnality.

One of Chiara Mandalà's letters mentioned "the happiness of the body." I wonder what a happy body might mean to a woman. If happiness is attainable only by mortifying and torturing one's own flesh, is it really possible to speak of a choice that's been freely made? From what we understand of Clare of Assisi through her writings and the way she lived—her stubborn, lifelong faith, forever tied to a decision she made as a girl—she would never have gone back on her word to her divine spouse or to herself. And yet the nuns say that at a certain point she had talked about wanting to go to Morocco, where several Franciscan friars had been martyred.

They add that her journey would have had the singular goal of achieving martyrdom. But is it irreverent to imagine something else behind her wish to go to Morocco?

We know that when she began her vocation, Clare thought she would take the word of God out to the people, just like Francis. Which meant she would have traveled through towns busying herself with the sick—not just the nuns whom she cared for so affectionately, but the lame, the blind, victims of the plague, the downtrodden who moved about on the peripheries of the world of the rich in Assisi. There's nothing heretical or unwholesome about a nun's sincere wishes to fulfill her vocation. Do I go too far if I suggest she might have even enjoyed getting on a boat and traveling to the Holy Land to see with her very own eyes the grotto where Christ was born, as her mother Ortolana had done? To kneel before the manger in which the *mammolo*—the Christ child—was warmed by the breath of a donkey and a cow? What would it have meant to her to gaze on horizons far from the restricted, cloistered space of the little convent of San Damiano? Was this a natural, legitimate desire, or a diabolical temptation, as the Fathers of the Church would have us believe?

Can we rule out the possibility that Clare wanted to leave the prison she chose and had once longed for, a prison that perhaps over time became too familiar?—only because, as legend has it, she became paralyzed and lost the movement of her legs from the time she was thirty until her death at fifty-nine? Freedom is not just about exercising one's will; it's not simply refusing to obey the rules or making mischief. There's also the freedom of curiosity, of discovery, of knowledge, of exchange, of wandering. That's where doubt sets in. Isn't it possible that her sickness was a pitiless, exaggerated act of renunciation, as she suppressed entirely legitimate feelings that others considered dangerous and illicit, diabolical and presumptuous? Is it disrespectful to think this? Is that why her legs were paralyzed? Why not her heart, her brain, her hands? It's as if she wanted to punish herself by turning against those very limbs that had prodded her to disobey.

Was her plan to preach and spread God's word no more than the desire to articulate the conventional formulas of the Church, within which her own thoughts were already confined? Or might it have sprung from that marvelous and most human of longings: to meet new people, visit unknown places, converse with strangers, possibly converting them to her faith through example and argument? Doesn't the liberty of man consist in movement and dialectic as well? Exactly, and I seem to hear Chiara Mandalà's voice saying yes, the liberty of *man*, a man who even grammatically constitutes himself as the center of the universe. But not woman, who is always derived from him: an appendix, a creature constantly in danger, needing to be guided, controlled, protected.

Clare spent the twenty-nine years of her illness ceaselessly spinning cotton and silk to decorate the altar coverings she sent to churches in Assisi. Without ever tiring, without ever complaining about her terrible paralysis. Was it just out of obedience and resignation, or was it a necessary penance so she wouldn't succumb to temptation? And what if accentuating the punitive nature of that passionate decision was the only way of controlling her situation? Was she perhaps at risk of becoming arrogant? Was it only to keep her hands busy that she dedicated herself so completely to embroidery? What if it was a way of turning deaf ears to a body that had to become crippled, and had to remain that way? A body held at bay through punishments, deprived of nourishment, mistreated, humiliated. What could they have been whispering about, those bodily members of a vigorous young girl who loved life, their voices firmly silenced? What could that determined, mortified little body have been saying in the mute language of desire: a body restrained with force, beaten down by fasting and penance? What was it saying that Clare simply didn't want to hear? Why did she carry this mysterious illness around with her for twenty-nine years?

What if instead those legs had demonstrated their autonomy, if those feet accustomed to going a thousand times from the kitchen to the chapel, from the chapel to the cloister, from the cloister to the dormitory, from the dormitory to the chapel, had calmly taken themselves toward that great door, closed and barred? And if those bare, callused feet had suggested to her that she leave, defying the cold and the rain and looking in the face the very world she had chosen to serve? Is it impertinent or disrespectful to think this of a saint? And yet it seems to me that this saint refused to understand what her poor, mistreated body was trying to tell her. What if those legs, still robust and young, were turned to stone so they couldn't speak out? Since the cloister is an inalienable destiny, it was essential that one choose that destiny and make it one's own in the most ferocious, most glorious manner possible, so transforming constraint into a virtue, imprisonment into sovereignty. Is that what Clare of Assisi wanted for herself?

JULY 5. The popes who reigned during Clare's lengthy sojourn in the convent all avoided confirming her Rule for her new order of Poor Clares, the first such rule ever written by a woman. One that, while timidly rejecting any hierarchy within the convent, refused all gifts and money from the outside, regardless of whether they came from the pope or a lay benefactor. The popes' reluctance nonetheless made sense: if nuns were supposed to be cloistered and forbidden to leave for any reason, if they were prohibited from working or begging for alms, how would they survive? Who would bring them food and provide them with life's necessities? Hence the need to ensure them some income, and thus property and resources. But property, as Saint Francis taught, has to be defended: with gates, keys, strongholds; with guard dogs, fences, sentinels. Property must be protected, and that's exactly what Clare didn't want. No property and nothing to defend. A nun should own only the clothes on her body, and that should be enough. She shouldn't even own food. She should support herself by working with her hands and asking for just a bite to eat in exchange. This was the freedom Francis proposed for his friars, and that Clare wanted for her nuns: the spectacular, terrible liberty of being naked in the world.

In his remarkable book *Most Exalted Poverty*, the philosopher Giorgio Agamben explores a different route. Francis sought to exercise what he saw as the natural right of using things that belonged to others, thus opening up to debate the very notion of property itself. Francis's arguments involving the "state of exception" present a form of communism in the making that demolishes the right to possession: "the Friars inverted the state of exception by making it absolute. Under normal circumstances, when men are under the jurisdiction of positive law, they don't have a right to use—only permission to use. But in states of extreme necessity, positive law is superseded by the return to and recuperation of natural law. . . . Thus, what is normal for others, becomes for the friars the exception: what is an exception for others becomes for them a way of life." A way of life that embodies, in simple terms, their "radical estrangement from law and liturgy."

In deciding to follow Christ in his extreme poverty, Clare and Francis renounced every form of possession for themselves and their successors. They were not interested in pursuing the notion of the use of anything as a right. But they did adhere to property held in common almost as though it were a right. Agamben writes that the Franciscan Bonaventure argued in 1269 that a papal bull by Gregory IX had created the basis for separating ownership from use. Bonaventure used the bull to establish for the friars that while "property may not be possessed, neither communally nor individually . . . [they could] enjoy the use of tools, books, and other things as necessary." And as Agamben goes on to explain, "Just as in Roman law, the son of the family [*filius familias*] can receive from his father a piece of property [*peculiam*], which he may use but not own, so the Friars are children and sons [*parvuli et filiifamlius*] of the pope, who likewise owns things that they may use."

All in all, to say along with the Franciscans that the air and sun and water belong to everyone and that everyone can enjoy them is to say that private property such as land, fields, vineyards, orchards, castles, palaces, kitchens, rooms, insofar as they are given by God, really is—or should be— at the disposal of everyone who wants to enjoy it. This is even more revolutionary and destabilizing than one might think, as Agamben points out. "Similarly, in Roman law those things that don't belong to anyone—such as shells that wash up on the shore, or wild animals—are called 'res nullius.' But since the first person who gathers or captures them becomes *ipso facto* their owner, it's evident that such things that seem to lie outside the law only presuppose the act of appropriation that sanctions their ownership." And he concludes, "This is why the Franciscans had to insist on the 'expropriative' character of poverty. And this too is why they refused to become creatures of possession, or an *animus possidenti*, reserving for themselves the use of things that were not their own. Yet as they became more and more involved in juridical entanglements, they were eventually overpowered and defeated."

JULY 12. I dreamed about a figure dressed in white silk, who led a barefoot little girl by the hand. They seemed to be walking on a carpet made of butterflies. A flying carpet, light and gleaming and radiant. Her tiny feet were red and swollen. His were large and enclosed within two golden slippers. When they were closer, I realized that he was the pope, and she was Clare. Ah, it's Innocent IV! I said to myself in my dream, that gentle pope who went to find her when she was gravely ill, and they were fearing for her life. "And Messer Innocent the Pope came to visit her when she was seriously ill," says Suor Philippa. "And then she said to the sisters, 'My children, praise God, since heaven and earth are not sufficient to contain all the goodness I have had from God, since today I have received him in the holy Sacrament.'"

Clare's relationship with the popes was a curious and contradictory one. She could be obsequious, respectful, and devout, but also disobedient, subversive, and independent. "She could never be persuaded, neither by the pope nor by Bishop Hostiensis, to accept possessions of any kind." Suor Philippa, as usual, is our guide. The pope was invoking the Fourth Lateran Council, which had mandated that new religious orders should adopt pre-existing rules like the Benedictine Rule—a Rule permitting goods such as dowries to be brought into convents. Clare didn't want to depart from the words of Jesus, who said, "Go, sell all you have and give it to the poor, then come and follow me!" That's where the contradictions began—contradictions that endured as long as she lived.

How many popes tried to get her to change her mind! Innocent III, Honorius III, Gregory IV, Innocent IV. To say nothing of all the cardinals. But Clare "could not be persuaded," and she finished with a victory, at least a victory that lasted as long as she was still alive. As Chiara Giovanna Cremaschi writes—herself a Poor Clare—Pope Innocent III was "a great pontiff open to the signs of the times, capable of understanding and blessing the novelty of Franciscan evangelism." He granted the Poor Clares the *Privilegium paupertatis* or the Privilege of Poverty. But Innocent wouldn't approve the much more encompassing Rule for the Order of the Women of San Damiano.

Change was afoot in Italy around the year 1200, especially in north-central Italy, where Cremaschi notes, "groups of women called to lives of contemplation and communal poverty had begun to spring up." The proliferation of such communities created problems for the Church. In 1218 Pope Honorius III would entrust his representative in Italy, Cardinal Ugolino di Segni, with leading an inquest designed to channel all those "scattered rivulets into a great river of female convents, to be merged under the solicitous and timely concerns of the Cardinal, who would begin immediately to impose order on spontaneity and difference."

As the cardinal would go on to inform the pope, the women had chosen a lifestyle that was based on two fundamental principles: a commitment to communal poverty that entailed owning "nothing under the sun," and the privilege of exemption. Or in Cremaschi's words, "independence from bishops and the right to appeal directly to the Apostolic See, which absolved them from having to pay duties, tolls, tithes, and any other taxes because of their poverty. In compensation they would guarantee their loyalty to the Rule of Saint Benedict as laid out in the orders of the Fourth Lateran Council, which obliged new forms of religious life to observe a pre-existing rule."

Ugolino di Segni, who would become Pope Gregory IX, was a learned man and a good strategist. But he followed the rules and was concerned by the rising number of groups dedicated to poverty. He was especially worried about the large numbers of women throughout Europe gathering in informal communities, who pledged themselves to chaste and impoverished lives free from papal control. Solicitous about doing his research, he felt compelled to go in person to Assisi to understand exactly what was going on there. On Easter Sunday of 1220, he presented himself at the convent of San Damiano to meet Clare. Cardinal Ugolino "was fascinated by the personality and spiritual stature of the young woman who was so direct in her dealings with him," as Chiara Giovanna Cremaschi put it. Despite his admiration, in the years following his visit, the cardinal did everything he could to "channel those monasteries created with the specific intent of living in radical poverty into the riverbed of what he would call his own order."

Thus began an intense struggle, full of injunctions and resistance, that would endure for years. "Some convents sought to embrace the Rule that Saint Francis had written for Saint Clare—the *Forma vivendi* or Form of life," writes Cremaschi, "and the nuns who had already experienced the new evangelical path of San Damiano started traveling to other convents to help institute it elsewhere, as is evident from the canonization proceedings." Innocent IV, however, confirmed a more restrictive rule for women, according to which convents would be obliged to possess sufficient property to guarantee their survival. The absolute poverty called for by Francis and Clare set off alarm bells within the Church, which wanted nothing to do with this radical plan—one that deprived monastic communities of any security in the future, while granting them enormous independence in the present, a prospect that left ecclesiastical authorities uneasy.

Clare fought like a tiger for her Rule to be officially approved. The popes went back and forth for years, intimating that they weren't exactly in disagreement with her, while never ratifying her order. The approval arrived shortly before Clare died, with Cardinal Rinaldo of Jenne becoming the first to approve a Rule written by a woman. A Rule that was confirmed by a papal bull from Innocent IV on August 9, 1253. Clare died on August 11.

The process of her canonization began in October of that year. In the meantime, Alexander IV had succeeded Innocent as pope. It was a trial that couldn't end quickly enough, rushed along by the need to change or at least mitigate Clare's Rule moments after it had been approved. It's clear that they wanted to get rid of an inconvenient personality, who had constantly disputed the monastic norms dictated from above. At the same time, they were surprised and flattered by the immense numbers of new believers who were breathing new life into the Church. That's why there was such a hurry to appoint an icon who was already venerated by the people. Clare's sainthood would transform her, once and for all, into the property of the Church—removing her from the hands of its most ardent adversaries.

Even today, in an Italy that has forgotten Clare's prophetic words, the papacy continues to practice the politics of a great state that both appeases and controls. But lately someone has been gumming up the works: Pope Francis I, the new pontiff who has come from faraway Argentina to stick his nose into the Vatican Bank and into the networks of power of the Holy See. And he does so with irony and impertinence, bringing in a burst of fresh air that reminds one of Francis and Clare of Assisi.

Pope Francis kneels down to wash the feet of young men incarcerated in Naples. I look at the photos that show him stooped over, gentle and patient, as he holds in his hand the perfectly clean heel of an inmate, a boy stunned by this unusual gesture. I see his tattooed foot and the pope delicately lifting it to immerse it in fresh water. I can't make out the tattoo. Might it be a dragon? A moving train? A butterfly? The pope doesn't stop to consider the small design on the inmate's skin. He's delicately immersed his foot in the shimmering waters of the basin. I can imagine the boy's timidity, his surprise, but also perhaps a sense of empowerment. Might he also be a little ashamed of that tiny drawing on his skin? Was it a mermaid or something like that? Can a pope hold in his hands a tattoo of a mermaid, with naked breasts and the tail of a fish? In a gesture of Franciscan humility, the pope pretends not to notice it. Gracefully bowed down before the boy, he lifts the bare foot out of the water and dries it off with a clean towel.

Madonna Clare would certainly never have encountered a mermaid tattooed onto the foot of one of her sisters, not even one of her serving women. These were girls from the countryside, with muscular arms, faces reddened by the sun, large tough feet accustomed to going without shoes. The young abbess could certainly have seen a scar close up, whatever might be left of a finger almost completely sliced off by a mishandled scythe. But not a mermaid. Though I'm sure she wouldn't have been scandalized if she had. She would have gently kissed that foot with the grace of one who welcomes the humble. So severe with the rich, so tolerant of those who had nothing.

JULY 21. Did the nuns have books at San Damiano? No one ever talks about books. But convents certainly had libraries.

Where else would the readings that accompanied meals otherwise consumed in silence have come from? Did they read stories of the lives of the saints, men and women alike? Figures from the Catholic world, for sure, but from more recent times as well as long ago? Who knows if the striking letter by the Carthaginian martyr Vibia Perpetua found its way to Assisi—a woman in love with her faith, who decided to abandon husband and son to accept the martyrdom inflicted on her by the Roman Empire in an era when it was illegal to be a Christian?

We are in Carthage in the year 203. Vibia Perpetua, who has recently given birth to a baby boy, is in the prison reserved for disloyal Roman subjects by the Emperor Septimus Severus. She is joined by Felicity, the wife of her servant, who is nine months pregnant. Perpetua was denounced and put on trial for civil disobedience. She belongs to a well-off, educated family. One of her brothers had already been baptized, but he managed to be in hiding at the moment of the arrest. With these two women are three other young Christian men: Saturninus, Revocatus, and Secondulus. The magistrates ask them to renounce their faith in Christ. If they do so, their lives will be saved. But none of them backs down, and calmly, courageously, they prepare for martyrdom.

During her months in prison, Perpetua kept a diary, miraculously preserved, albeit fragmentary. She speaks often of her dreams. And she writes about her father, who is so worried and upset that he constantly visits her in prison to persuade her to renounce her faith for the sake of her family, but especially for her son, who has just been born and who needs her. Perpetua's writing style is clear, knowing, straightforward. She shows a familiarity with the classics that very few women then had: "When we were still under legal surveillance, my father, out of his great love for me, insisted on opposing my arguments and sought to weaken my resolve, I said to him, 'Father, do you see that container over there, something like a jug or a vase, do you see it?' and he said, 'Yes, I see it.' And I said to him, 'How can you refer to a vase if not with its proper name, a vase, since it's obviously a vase?' And he was unable to reply. Then I said, 'Just as you can call that vase only a vase, so I too can't call myself anything but what I am, a Christian.' Irate, my father threw himself upon me as though he wanted to tear out my eyes. But he was only upset; and vanquished, he went off, along with the sophistries of the devil."

Today we would call this nominalism, thanks to John Locke. Do things exist apart from their names? If it weren't for linguistic conventions, how could we ever understand one another? If we didn't give a name to God, would we have any consciousness of him? Returning to the question: Do things exist outside of the names we give them? This is the unsettling problem that has kept so many philosophers awake at night. And it clashes with the certainties of faith—a faith that has no need of proof but thrives on deep and absolute feeling.

And what if instead we give a name to something that doesn't exist? For example, if we call a creature a unicorn— not found in the real world, but in dreams and art and iconography (I'm thinking of a beautiful painting by Gustave Moreau of a unicorn standing upright on all fours in a dense thicket of blackberry bushes)—can we then say that unicorns exist to the same degree as a zebra or a horse? After all, words give bodies to things, but even thoughts and emotions don't occupy a place in our consciousness until we name them. If I say that I'm a Christian, I've given a space and a linguistic place to my feelings and thoughts; I've transformed an abstract concept into a body that's real and concrete. If that body is united to thought and feeling and is prepared to die or obliterate itself in order to remain faithful to its linguistic identity, the circle is complete.

Perpetua's nominalism is not separate from reality; it serves neither to comfort nor to distract. Let's listen to her story, so logical and realistic and raw: "After a few days, we were led into the prison, and I was frightened because I had never known such darkness. What an evil day! Intense heat, human bodies pressed together, extortions by the soldiers. Above all I was tormented with worry for the fate of my child. Then Tertius and Pomponius, the consecrated deacons who oversaw us, bribed the guards to take us for a few hours to a better and cooler part of the prison. Once we left the cell, we were able to move more easily. I nursed my son, who was suffering from lack of nourishment. I talked to my mother, I consoled my brother, and I entrusted to them my child. I was exhausted to see how they had worn themselves out for my sake. Such were my terrifying thoughts for many days. Then I received permission to keep my child with me in prison. And instantly I felt better, freed of my worries and concerns for him. At once prison became for me a palace, and there was no other place where I would have chosen to be."

The account reveals a young woman, decisive but not blinded by fanaticism. A woman who suffers and knows how to describe her suffering in straightforward terms, a young mother preoccupied with the fate of her son—whom she is still nursing—and altogether humane in the way that she grieves for the heartache she is causing her family. But despite all this, when they ask her, "Are you a Christian?" she responds, "I'm a Christian." Just like a vase that can't be called anything but a vase, or a horse that can't be called anything but a horse. Even if the word implies a universal concept, the person exists in the here and now: as a body, with her arms, her head of dark black hair bound behind her neck in a knot, her stocking-clad feet and shoulders covered by a lovely shirt made from the cotton fabrics of Egypt, now dirty and torn after weeks in prison.

Her brother who remains at liberty asks Perpetua to pray for a vision: "My brother then said to me, 'Lady, my sister, you are now greatly blessed: enough to ask for a vision to be shown to you, so you will know whether you will have to suffer until death or if this is an evil that shall pass.'" Perpetua thought for a bit and then promised him, "Tomorrow I'll let you know, my brother." And she prepared herself for a night of prophetic dreams.

"I saw a bronze ladder, marvelously long and narrow that thrust up into heaven, and you could only climb up one person at a time. And alongside the ladder were all kinds of metal objects: swords, lances, hooks, daggers, javelins, arranged in such a way that if someone climbed without paying attention or without looking around, he would have been cut to pieces, his flesh pierced by sharp metal. Beneath the ladder lay coiled a serpent of prodigious size, threatening all who climbed, making them terrified to go on. But Saturus went first (later he would unhesitatingly offer to take our place: he had filled us with courage, and when we were arrested he was not there). He reached the top of the ladder, turned around and said to me, 'Perpetua, I'll wait for you, but be careful that the snake doesn't bite you.' And I said, 'He won't wound me, in the name of Christ.' And it seemed to me that the serpent below, as though it was almost frightened by me, slowly bowed down, almost becoming the first step on the ladder. So I stepped on him and went on up.'" An extraordinary effort of Perpetua: she's aware that the sharp iron could cut her skin, she knows about the serpent who could tear her to pieces. But she places her foot on the serpent's head as though it was the first step of the ladder. And she starts to climb.

What does Vibia Perpetua find at the top of the ladder? "I saw an immense garden, in the middle of which stood a tall man with white hair. He was dressed as a shepherd, and was milking his sheep, and many thousands of people all around him were dressed in luminous white. He lowered his head, gazed at me and said, 'Welcome, my child.' He called me to him and gave me, or so it seemed, a mouthful of cheese that he was preparing. I took it with both my hands and ate it, and all those around him cried out, 'Amen!' At the sound of that word, I woke up, still savoring the taste of something indefinably sweet."

Perpetua's dream is very similar to the dream Clare had about Francis. In both we have a ladder, a maternal male waiting at the top of the steps, and the gift of food, sweet to the taste. The food isn't milk, but it's made from milk. By Clare's time, almost a millennium had passed since that long-ago dream of Vibia Perpetua in the year 203. But it seems that the symbolic language of the Church had not changed.

When her family arrives in the prison the next day, Vibia tells the dream to her brother, and he understands that "she was destined to encounter death, and we began to hope no more in the world." In the meantime, word gets out that the five confessed Christians will be sentenced to death. Her father returns to find his daughter: "My daughter, please take pity on my white hairs!" he begs her, and when she refuses, he insists: "Show your father compassion, if I'm worthy of being called your father. With these hands I carried you in the flower of your youth. I favored you over all your brothers. Don't disgrace me before the eyes of these men! Gaze on your brothers, look upon your mother and your aunt, look at your own child, who will not survive your death. Don't persist in such stubbornness, or you will destroy us all." Then the father moves from familial tenderness to more social preoccupations. "If something happens to you, none of us will be able to speak openly or freely any longer." In addition to worrying about losing his daughter, Perpetua's father is also concerned for the future of the family. With a child condemned to death, he won't be able to say what he thinks anymore, but he will be under continual surveillance and singled out as the father of a criminal.

Curiously, it's the father, never the mother, who keeps returning to implore his daughter, at one point even tearing the hairs out of his beard one by one. "Make the sacrifice, daughter," he insists, "have pity on your child!"—a sacrifice to be fulfilled with Perpetua's renunciation of her Christian identity. The governor Hilarianus, who had received judicial powers from the late proconsul Minucius Timinianus, also arrives to persuade Perpetua to reject her faith: "Spare the venerable years of your father, save the childhood of your son! Fulfill the rite for the fortune of the emperor!" he urges her out of kindness. But Perpetua remains calm. "I won't do it." And Hilarianus, incredulous, asks her again: "Are you thus a Christian?" Perpetua answers, loudly and with pride: "I am a Christian." Afterwards she will write in her journal, "The governor then sentenced us all to death in the arena, to be mauled by the animals. And joyfully we returned to our prison."

With this, the full impact of the condemnations becomes clear. The judges felt they had the duty to punish the disobedient, just as Creon did with Antigone, knowing they would lose face if the law were not applied. But at the same time, they feared the consequences of such a judgment. It escaped no one that these Christians were examples to be admired, given their courage and quiet acceptance of death. Everyone knew their crimes were crimes of thought. They'd done nothing evil, other than declare themselves Christians in a world ruled by pagans. Everyone knew it was only a question of power, the power of a state religion seeking to impose uniformity at all costs. But at the very moment in which it exacted the penalty, it turned the enemy into a hero.

In the meantime, Felicity gives birth to a son. They immediately take him away along with Perpetua's child, and give him to his grandparents. Now Felicity too is ready to die. The five of them will be conducted into the arena, in the midst of the lions. The Christian community trembles, asking why Emperor Septimus Severus, who until now has shown himself relatively tolerant toward the followers of Christ, is tightening the knot. The answer lies precisely in Christianity's increasing popularity and its widespread appeal. As the war heats up, the emperor decides to become more rigorous with the "unfaithful." If they renounce the word of Christ, fine; otherwise there is only death. And it will be a spectacular death. The public must have a great spectacle to watch.

It's said that the two women were the first to be thrust into the arena. The starving beasts threw themselves onto them both, but they targeted the young Felicity first, drawn perhaps to the smell of her breast milk. We have to remember that she had just given birth, and her breasts were full. They say that when a lion tore Felicity's garments with his paw, her friend Perpetua immediately covered her back up so she wouldn't be seen naked by the public. But another lion in the meantime closed in on Felicity and, with a single bite, broke her neck. Holding her in his mouth, he whipped her around as hunters do when they want to make sure they've killed their prey. The public, so it is said, took pity on the poor young mother. In the meantime, the lion began circling the arena, dragging the bleeding cadaver around in a show of feline pride. Paralyzed with horror, the spectators watched as the beast eventually went off into a corner to devour the body, while the other lions slowly gathered around. At this point, a judge appointed by the emperor cried out that the will of the gods had been fulfilled. The other four Christians knelt to pray. And the guards incited the beasts to take out their rage on them. The carnage lasted for quite a few hours, according to the chronicles. The audience did not leave until the last of the condemned was torn to pieces, and the lions, satiated, hunkered down on one side, their mouths dripping with human blood.

In an era of abstractions and formalities, the writings of Vibia Perpetua stand out for their clarity, their rationality, their honesty and conviction. It's a shame that they only amount to a few pages. But they are extraordinary pages, among the most expressive and beautiful that Christian literature has ever produced. It may seem hard to believe, but evidently because they were written by a woman, they were condemned to be canceled from the historical record—even the historical record of the church. Thanks to a few passionate scholars such as the medievalist Peter Dronke, they have now been brought to light.

JULY 24. What would I do without books? My house is full of them, but I never have enough. I'd love it if days were thirty-six hours long just so I could read for pleasure. I own books of all shapes and sizes: books that fit in my pocket, books that fit in my suitcase, in my purse, on my shelf, on my coffee table. And I'm always carrying one with me. I never know if I might find a moment to read; if they make me wait at the post office or the doctor's, I'll take out my book and start reading. When my nose is in a book I never get tired of waiting. As Ortega y Gasset says, I make myself at "home" in a book, and it's difficult to unhouse me. I emerge with my eyes wide open. I consider reading to be the greatest, most reliable, most profound pleasure of my life.

I wonder if there were any books in the convent of San Damiano they would have considered pagan. Virgil, for example, for whom Odo, abbot of Cluny, burned with desire because of the beauty of his words and his splendid descriptions of nature. But beauty can be insidious, the abbot said to himself. And so one night, after having enjoyed reading Virgil at length, he was admonished in a dream. He dreamt that he was admiring a lovely vase, painted in beautiful colors. But while he was gazing at it, poisonous serpents crawled out, and he fled. So he divined that emotions brought on by beauty could be dangerous, that a man dedicated to God shouldn't be lingering over pages written by a pagan. A true Christian can't read texts that have nothing to do with Christianity without the risk of being misled. From that day on, Odo read only the sacred Scriptures and the writings of the Church Fathers, or so he declared.

The abbey of Cluny was famous for its learning, but also for its severity. Students had to learn Latin and Greek while repudiating the works of the great Latin and Greek poets. But Aristotle and Plato continued to enchant the clerics who knew how to read. Shamefully, secretively, they would occasionally venture to read the lyric poets who sang of wine and lust, like Alcaeus, or Anacreon. Who knows if they glanced now and then at Sappho, at Stesichorus, or Archilochus!

"His chaste soul was stained by his daily reading of the poets," Edmond Pognon says of Gervinus in *Daily Life in the Year 1000*. Future abbot of Saint-Riquier and a student of the school of Reims, Gervinus stopped reading the pagans after being warned against them, tossing out the Latin and Greek classics from his library that admittedly he had begun to love.

The life of the convent was regulated in such a way that it didn't leave any time for reading that wasn't carried out in public and therefore supervised. Curiously, in an era without clocks, time was observed with rigorous precision. Sundials existed back then, but they could only be found on high towers, too far away to see from home. Time was registered by the crowing of the rooster, the insistent pealing of bells, the firing of a cannon. Candles served to mark the passage of time when it was dark. Some candles lasted for an hour and others for three hours; one knew how much time had passed as long as they were still burning.

They calculated time the way the Romans did: twelve hours of day, twelve of night. Convents established four periods for their vigils, two before midnight, two after. The first hour corresponded with sunrise; the third signaled nine A.M., the sixth midday, the ninth the middle of the afternoon, and Vespers coincided with sunset. The hour of evening prayer was called Compline, and that of midnight "il Nottorno"— Nocturnes—while the 2:00 A.M. prayer was called "Mattutino" or little morning (Matins), and the one said at dawn, "Lauds."

During the canonization proceedings, Suor Benvenuta of Perugia emphasized Clare's dedication to the hours or vigils: "This witness said that the previously named mother Saint Clare was very assiduous about praying both day and night. And around midnight she would use certain signs to awaken the sisters without making any noise, so they could praise God." Silence was the rule, and we can imagine a barefoot Clare, one minute washing off her face in a small basin with a few drops of freezing water, the next running a wooden comb through her cropped hair, adjusting her head cover to secure it above her veil with a large pin, and then noiselessly dashing off to the other beds to awaken her sleeping sisters with a light touch on the shoulder.

Next, without making a sound, she would descend the stairs and open the door to the chapel. And then "she would light the lanterns in the church and would often ring the bell for Mattutino herself." The sisters would scurry about, barefoot and cold like Clare, rubbing their eyes and yawning—but putting their hands over their mouths because it wasn't polite to make the Lord think they weren't eager to pray to him. "And as for those sisters who didn't get up with the sound of the bells, she would call them using special gestures." After the sisters were counted, if someone was missing, Clare would quickly return to the dormitory above, approaching the cots to prod—a bit more energetically this time around—those nuns who were still sleeping peacefully, to make them go down to the chapel and pray.

Like a mother hen with baby chicks, Clare ran up and down those steep stairs of *pietra serena*, that lovely, rippled white and gray stone that is found around Assisi and with which the modest convent of San Damiano was built. She was never tired, never impatient. It was Francis who asked her when she was barely twenty-one, in 1215, to do him the great favor of being the abbess. She didn't want to. She was reluctant to assume any form of power. But she obeyed, as she always did; she obeyed this man whom she loved as a father and brother. Francis knew that Clare wouldn't abuse the power that was associated with running a convent. If anything, she seemed so nonplussed, so uninterested in the privilege that she treated it not as a boon but as one more duty, merely an opportunity to serve her sisters. All the nuns attest to her generosity, to her willingness to be always at their disposal and her desire to make them happy: "She was extremely humble, devout, sweet, and a great lover of poverty, with compassion for all the afflicted," reports Suor Philippa. And she adds: "Such was the sanctity of our holy mother's life and the honesty of her manners that neither I nor any of the other nuns could ever fully describe it."

The nuns simply couldn't understand why an abbess would behave like a servant. Not only was she an equal among equals, but she delighted in taking upon herself the most unpleasant and laborious tasks, staying on her feet when she needed to sleep, eating only what she had to in order to stay alive. This was entirely novel. The city was full of convents, and there was talk about how other abbesses behaved. Usually they were women from noble families who felt they had every right to mistreat their social inferiors, put on airs, impose high-handed rules of every kind, and be waited on as though they were queens. This is why the sisters of San Damiano so loved their Monna Chiara, with her extraordinary and surprising willingness to be helpful. Whose actions could only have come from a religious choice, precisely because *epsa*—"that lady"—belonged to a rich and noble family and could easily have acted like a snob, punishing and ordering the nuns around the way other abbesses did. But she never did anything like that.

When she really couldn't convince a sister to carry out her responsibilities—to pray, or fast, or stay awake, or work—she would kneel at her feet and implore the nun to "do her this one favor" and fulfill her obligations—or so the sisters said when they were asked as witnesses. This is even though it was within Clare's power to command and insist—not to mention to inflict punishment, had she wanted to. Punishment was considered not only legal, but essential. Pognon writes that children "raised within monasteries and destined to the monastic life were commonly whipped for any minor resistance to the rules," and "if a child did something bad a second time, he was put in chains, refused food, and often enclosed within a prison cell." Pognon is referring here to the situation in France and England, but it's not hard to imagine that in its universalizing zeal, the Church would have proposed the same rules and the same punishments for whoever opposed it, wherever they were. Corporal punishment was considered a valuable part of children's education, especially for girls. In England, one must wait until 1891 before a law is passed that—far from abolishing corporal punishment—recommends only that such punishments be moderated, and only with respect to husbands faced with disobedient wives. Rules that would affect boys and girls would not be on the books for many more years.

"The punitive mentality of the middle ages is especially evident in Dante's *Divine Comedy*, where the configuration of divine order is strictly analogous to the human one," writes Stefania Romanelli in her article "Punishment in the Middle Ages." "Crimes were understood to be sins, a perspective that emphasizes the primacy of the subjective aspect of criminal action. Categorizing sins as acts of incontinence, injustice, violence and fraud has much in common with modern distinctions between crimes of passion and crimes of violence, between born criminals and habitual ones. Punishment could be either temporary or permanent. The first kind expresses a concept of punishment that facilitates improvement and change. The second sees punishment as retributive, exacting the criterion of the *contrappasso*, which asserts that the perpetrator must suffer in equal measure the evil he has inflicted on others."

Contrappasso is the ancient law of "an eye for an eye." Even today vendetta is rooted, ever resilient, in the human heart. "Dante closely connects the punishment to the underlying causes of the crime," continues Romanelli, "linking together the psychological factors that led to a criminal act, the consequences unleashed by that act, and the disciplinary sanctions imposed as a result of that act, so as to bring about the redemption of the condemned." An individual's relationship to his or her own body was experienced as an ongoing, ferocious war. The body was the kingdom of evil, which is why it had to be punished, repressed, guided, forced, censured, and often literally tortured by a tormented, tormenting conscience.

But whence this blind hatred of bodily pleasures? Is it unique to Christianity? The Cathars were certainly the most radical in this respect, among groups defiant of the Church. They opposed all the sacraments, recognizing only that of the "Consolamentum." A form of baptism for adults who had reached the age of consent, the rite liberated them from sin and served as their initiation into a life of renunciation and sacrifice. The Cathars rejected war and private property. They preached absolute equality among all people, irrespective of race, class difference, language, custom, age, or sex. They expected the Church and its priests to be as poor as Christ was, calling for the restoration of the apostolic life. Everyone could preach without limitations of any kind. Everyone had to support themselves through work. They rejected corporal punishment. They refused to tithe and pay taxes to secular powers. They believed that the spiritual world was created by God, while the world of flesh had its roots in the devil. That's why human beings had to constantly engage in a battle between body and soul. They discouraged marriage, even if they acknowledged that it was necessary for the conservation of the species; many simply thought that if the human race should become extinct it would be no great loss. Sexual relations were disapproved of, if not expressly prohibited. The body had to be made subject to the spirit. Fleshly appetites needed to be tamed, strangled, spent until all desire was simply annihilated. A true Cathar would gladly die of hunger.

JULY 29. And as for Waldus? That is, Peter Waldus of Lyon, founder of the Waldensians. There are some curious similarities between him and Saint Francis. Both belonged to wealthy merchant families, families that trafficked in precious cloths such as wool, cotton, and linen. Both men stripped themselves of their every possession, including their shoes, and clothed themselves in tunics to go out into the streets and preach the Gospel. Both considered including women in the practice of their apostolates, notwithstanding the prohibitions of the Church. Waldus was excommunicated during the Synod of Verona in 1184. In contrast, Francis engaged, successfully, in truly extraordinary acrobatics, remaining within the Church while criticizing it, upholding papal authority while advocating a return to the poverty of Christ. His diplomatic and political dexterity meant surrendering a great deal to the Church, while he preserved his autonomy with respect to his own thinking. So Francis had to yield on some things such as women's preaching, about which the popes were inflexible. Under no circumstances could nuns be allowed to go about preaching the word of God. They were supposed to stay shut up in the convent, and that was that.

Clare's sacrifice was even more painful. Politically astute as she was, she realized that the only smart thing to do was to accept what was imposed on her by the sheer fact of her gender, and carve out her own form of liberty within those constraints. A painful liberty, but real, and one lived with blinding intensity. Rather than complain and protest her fate, the prisoner made prison the place of her choice, a place for reflection, for passion and glory, and in the end she triumphed. She could leave her cell without even wanting to, as light on her feet as winged Mercury. And the space of isolation engendered in Clare a preference for privacy, and an attachment to forms of penance that tapped into the deepest meanderings of her psyche, into the dark light of solitary thought.

That said, one has to understand how harsh and difficult the practice of seclusion really was. An uphill climb, bristling with thorns and nails. And Clare came to know those nails and those thorns. But her piercing intelligence and instinct for liberty enabled her to transform her prison into a beloved home, representative of her choice, and of her martyrdom: a martyrdom she sought, and thus she did not suffer—despite the rebelliousness of a young, healthy body that protested, languished, consumed itself, cried out in protest. But Clare's will was adamantine. Throughout her lengthy confinement, she did not yield for one instant to discomfort, to fear, to sickness, to difficulties, to doubt. All we can do is admire her.

"She punished her body by wearing rough garments, on occasion having them made from the bristles of horsehair, or horsetail," testifies Suor Philippa. "And she wore a tunic and cape of coarse cloth." If pain is welcomed as the only means of expressing one's commitment to a way of life, then it will produce not suffering but divine pleasure and delight. Clare often said that disgusting odors would smell like lilies when you chose to turn the world of the senses upside down. The scratching of bristles can feel pleasant on the skin.

"She also said that the aforementioned Mother, holy Clare, before she became ill, was so abstemious that throughout all of Lent and again during the Lent of Saint Martin [between All Saints' Day and Christmas], she would eat only bread and water, except for on Sundays when she drank a little wine, when there was wine to be had." Precisely: the nuns of San Damiano never bought anything. Out of their own personal conviction, they never handled money. They lived on what they were given to eat, collected by the Franciscan friars or left at the convent's gate by peasants who knew they were indigent: bread, beans, fruit.

There was plenty of work to do in the convent, but it brought in no money. Clare embroidered the corporals that she would give to various churches, while other nuns tended to the garden and mended garments, but only for themselves. Had they been able to go out, they could have cared for the sick in exchange for something to eat; they could have worked the land in exchange for some fruit. Would hens have been laying eggs in the courtyard behind the kitchen? It's not clear; I haven't found any reference in the testimonies. Clare declared that they shouldn't own anything, not even a goat or a rooster. And Saint Francis, despite his love for animals, writes in his first rule for his friars, "I command of my friars, clerics and lay brothers, those who travel about and those who remain in one place, that for no reason can they maintain for themselves or for others any animals. Nor are they allowed to ride a horse unless forced to do so because of some infirmity or grave necessity."

There was a small orchard behind the rectory, although the nuns never thought of it as their property. In theory, anyone could have gone there to plant carrots or cabbage. Clare considered it like everything else in the convent: not the possession of any one person, but rather intended for whoever took a liking to it and wanted to spend time there. A place not to defend, but to share.

AUGUST 1. Once again, I dreamed of a young Clare, as she giggled and ran about. I heard her voice come bubbling up in a happy little laugh, if only for an instant. It was a joyous voice, like the trill of silver bells. I watched her jumping about with quick, light movements, like a happy bird. She seemed to be counting, as though she were playing hopscotch, jumping from one square to the next, etched onto the pavement with chalk: two, three, hop; five, six, hop, hop. Clare's biographers say nothing about her childhood. The only thing they mention is that she collected stones to put aside for counting her prayers. They say that she was quiet and never wanted to leave home. In other words, a child who by the time she was five was already a nun, already called to sanctity by the time she was nine.

In my dream she was alone but happy, absorbed in games that were not to be confused with prayers. Why must a female saint be born already saintly, while the lives of male saints before their conversion—many of them quite reprehensible—are talked about almost with complacency? They say that Francis was a reckless boy who loved fancy clothes and easy companions. He was good at singing and at playing games, someone who stood out in everything because of his expansive character and his competitiveness. And then he was called to his vocation, and everything changed. He abandoned his friends, his nice clothes, his family, and his inheritance, devoting himself to preaching and a vagabond life that took no stock of possessions. They say nothing about what led Clare to her choice of monasticism. It's not even a decision she was said to have made freely, but a destiny imposed by heaven.

It's always the winners who write History. In this instance, the winners were the clerics. Their point of departure was the assumption that women aren't capable of making decisions on their own. The only thing that drives them is fate, or at most a certain inclination, or character. But never an informed and conscious will that can decide its future. When Clare was eight years old, someone, perhaps even a loving God, had already decided that she would become a holy and sacrificial recluse. If it wasn't God the father who compelled her to a life of sanctity, perhaps then it was Saint Francis who infected her with his ideas. Doesn't this seem a trifle implausible? A woman's greatness should lie in her contradictions, her quest to understand the world and to form her own ideas. In what she reads, what she learns, how she changes and conquers herself; in her slow journey toward self-knowledge and which path she chooses to follow. What virtue is there in being born already perfect and holy?

A nun, however, was supposed to be a bride of Christ. It was repeated hundreds of times. And the enclosure of the convent was meant to prepare her for her final encounter with that most handsome, charming, and loving of husbands. Expected to preserve their integrity and dwell ignorant of the world, these recluses awaited their promised spouse, whose body was the only one they were allowed to desire. However, there was just one Christ, and many brides. They had to get used to the fact that they weren't his only beloved. One husband with many wives—happy and all in love, each one waiting for just a little attention. It never crossed anyone's mind to ask monks to consider themselves husbands of the Virgin Mary. They could adore her, but they were never referred to as her husbands. For Francis and his Franciscans, Christ was a brother. Where did the idea come from that nuns had to be brides rather than the sisters or daughters of Christ? It's generally thought that all Christians are children of God; hence Christ should be considered a brother. Why were they so adamant about turning women into his wives?

"To the esteemed and most holy virgin and lady Agnes, daughter of the most excellent and illustrious King of

Bohemia," writes Clare in one of her famous, beautiful letters to the great Agnes of Prague, who, promised in marriage to the Emperor Frederick II, chose the convent and enclosure instead. "For though You, more than others, could have enjoyed the magnificence, honor, and dignity of the world and could have been married to the illustrious Emperor with splendor befitting You and His Excellency, You have rejected all these things and have chosen with Your whole heart and soul a life of holy poverty and bodily want. Thus, you took a spouse of a more noble stock, Who will keep Your virginity ever unspotted and unsullied, the Lord Jesus Christ."

The bridegroom guarantees innocence and chastity, even if this groom is more than just an idea or symbol: he is a man, who knows how to touch and possess a woman: "Whom in loving, You are chaste; / in touching, You become more pure; / in embracing, You are a virgin; / Whose strength is more robust, / generosity more lofty, / Whose appearance is more handsome, / love more courteous, / and every kindness more refined."

At exactly the very moment when Clare makes carnal love a thing of metaphor and abstraction, she will return to its sensuality with even more urgency: "[Christ's] embrace already holds you; / [He] who has adorned Your breast with precious stones, / placed priceless pearls on Your ears, / surrounded You completely with blossoms / of springtime and sparkling gems / and placed on Your head / a golden crown as a sign of Your holiness." It's strange to listen to a Clare who was continually praising poverty as she imagines this elegantly dressed bride, outfitted in jewels and a crown, as though her husband were an apparition of the emperor rather than the impoverished Christ who carried a cross on his shoulders.

"The king will join you to himself in the heavenly bridal chamber where He is seated in glory on a starry throne," Clare writes in another letter to Agnes in her sweet, lyrical style, enhanced by quotes from the Bible. The theme of celestial matrimony is repeated ad infinitum in these four letters to Agnes that have survived. Clare's shift in the second letter from formal to informal address makes us think that she may have written other letters, now unfortunately lost: "[Considering] of little value the offers of an imperial marriage, instead as someone zealous for the holiest poverty, in a spirit of great humility and the most ardent love, you have held fast to the footprints of Him to whom you merited to be joined in marriage." A matrimony that justly unites two souls, never two bodies. "Draw me after you, / let us run in the fragrance of your perfumes, / O heavenly Spouse!" Clare writes to Agnes in the fourth letter, imitating the sensually poetic tones of the biblical Song of Songs. "I will run and not tire, / until You bring me into the wine-cellar, / until Your left hand is under my head, / and Your right hand will embrace me happily, / You will kiss me with the happiest kiss of Your mouth." The biblical text reads, "Leva eius sub capite meo, et dextera illius amplexabitur me": His left hand is under my head, and his right hand shall embrace me (Canticles 2:6).

I don't know if Christ would have approved of this multiplication of brides. He had neither fiancée nor wife. And yet this was the interpretation given by the Church: every nun had to make herself one with him through the bond of matrimony. And she had to live harmoniously with the other brides as though they were all one peaceful, heavenly family. Nonetheless, in the writings of other mystics this strange relationship comes to light in the form of a disguised, if restrained jealousy, with only the pretext of spontaneous and natural exclusivity. In her Dialogue of 1503, Domenica da Paradiso (1473–1553) goes to the extent of observing that since Christ is her husband, God must be her father-in-law. Such candor helps us realize how complicated these families with relatives in heaven really were, prompting sentiments that could feel quite arbitrary. Didn't the Church consider marriage monogamous? Didn't it prohibit even the thought of infidelity? Why attribute to Jesus this abundance of brides?

But it's all just about symbols, one might say; and after all, the Middle Ages were strongly attached to symbols. Yet symbols have their own consistency, and there's always some rationale behind them; they're not just castles fashioned in the air. Why would men dedicated to God be called brothers, while women were called wives? In what, exactly, did their relationship with the sacred consist? Why such talk of marriage if it was supposed to be a relationship between a brother and sister? We can have many siblings but only one spouse— isn't that what the Church teaches? Why hand young virgins over to a celestial husband who had other wives, and who would never give them children? Would Christ have agreed with this symbolic polygamy that was attributed to him, even if only in platonic fashion? The writings of women mystics show that nuns took their wedding with Christ seriously. They accepted in good faith what they were told when they were young girls: that after a long wait they would finally arrive at their wedding day with Jesus. And they were convinced it would be a marriage of both body and spirit. It turned them into lifelong virgins with no prospect of motherhood, forever awaiting that marvelous sexual union as the culmination of a solitary lifetime of sacrifice and seclusion.

The mystic Caterina Paluzzi (1573–1645) refers explicitly to these "other brides" of Christ. As a young girl she was curious and hungry for knowledge. Since no one wanted to teach her how to read and write, she invented imaginary teachers for herself with whom she would converse. When she discovered the letters of Saint Catherine of Siena, she became a devoted follower, joining the Dominican order as a tertiary when she was nineteen. She engaged in a lengthy correspondence with Cardinal Federico Borromeo. She founded a convent for Dominican women in Morlupo, near Rome. In her autobiography, she describes a vision in which she finds herself in a lovely garden alongside other brides of Christ. She exhibits neither jealousy nor feelings of rivalry, but relates how Christ, as though he'd forgotten about the presence of the other women, approached only Caterina so he might "wait on her." "I told him that it was up to me to serve him, and not for him to wait on me," reports Caterina, "because in serving me he would only be abasing himself. In answering me, he seemed to say that he wasn't abasing himself in any way, but that his very greatness and delight consisted in serving others." When Caterina registers surprise, Christ insists: "Not only do I serve those whom I love, but I respect them as mothers, I love them as sisters, I enjoy them as wives."

"Oh my bridegroom, so handsome, so lovely, so tender and patient, so gracious and kind," says Maria Maddalena de' Pazzi (1566–1607), a mystic from an aristocratic family who entered a convent of Carmelite nuns when she was sixteen. She was a talented speaker and people came from everywhere to listen to her preach. But she did not know how to write. So the nuns would gather around her when she spoke, each one committing to memory a section of her discourse so they could transcribe it. As chronicles recount, she would usually preach while standing utterly still, her eyes closed. Other times, overtaken by frenzy, she would run about in the courtyard of the convent as she spoke, and the nuns had trouble keeping up with her. "Next to my spouse I am nonexistent, I am nothing, and without you I cannot, I do not, want to want any other being," she would repeat.

Brigida Morello, a mystic born in Rapallo in 1610, was married, but upon becoming a widow at twenty-three, she took a vow of chastity, opening a school for young girls and writing a number of books. She recounts that one day while she was working, she saw a light and felt something heavy on her breast. She looked up to discover that "it was my Lord. I saw him standing there, a naked infant, a tiny *putto* who had just been born, and this child caressed me while he lay lovingly stretched out on my breast, over my heart, on my shoulder, near my face. I couldn't move my arms or anything else, and these expressions of humility and love would have seen me buried in ashes but unable to do anything else whatsoever. I surrendered myself completely to my Lord." Seductive visions emerge, modest miracles of imaginations in confinement. Not only is the celestial groom transformed into a newborn who plays with Brigida and whose sweet caresses on her face, her breast, her shoulders are utterly welcome. She also writes that when receiving communion in the chapel each morning, she would immediately hear her Lord speaking to her through the sacred host, saying with a gentle voice, "Satisfy yourself, this is my milk." And she is so moved and excited that "she felt herself turning completely to liquid."

Often these excessively sensual brides attracted the attention of ecclesiastical authorities, who denounced them to the Holy Inquisition. Veronica Giuliani (1660–1727) was one of them. The youngest of seven siblings from a well-off family, she wrote that she had played at being a mother when she was only four, staging dramatic breastfeedings of the infant Jesus. At nineteen, she closed herself up among the Capuchin nuns of Città di Castello. It did not take much for her to go into ecstasy, prompting the other nuns' concern and admiration. A fanatical young Jesuit accused her of heresy, and her punishments included being forced to lick her own excrement and to swallow insects. She was locked up and later released. She wrote a total of 22,000 pages in her diary, in which the most common invocation is this: "Lord, the more crosses there are, the more suffering there is!" And she beseeched the other nuns, "Suffer, suffer so that among your torments you will find love." Addressing herself to Jesus, she would ask, "But who am I for you?" And he would respond, "You are my house, my refuge." To which she would respond, "You are my delight, my only good, spouse of my soul." And she continued excitedly, "Then my bridegroom bowed before me, and he kissed me, and I did the same to him."

One is struck by the sensuality of these descriptions of mystical brides in love. Is this why their writings were censured and left to languish in the drawers of convents for centuries? "I am crazy, crazy for love," Veronica writes of Christ her bridegroom. "I seek to become ever more crazed, and my amorous madness will make me cry out ever more forcefully. This suffering for love gives me life." And then, in tones even more provocative and lyrical: "Dying, I live so I don't die of love. Living, I die so that I don't find love. I love not knowing how to love. Love calls me and I wait to hear him; Love speaks so I can understand."

Such sentiments hover on the verge of forbidden eros. But really, what can you expect from a girl who was just a teenager? She had been enclosed in a prison for life, promised the embrace of a bridegroom whom she could meet only in her dreams, constrained to sublimate every erotic or amorous instinct to the monotony and torture of anticipation: "Even if

God sent me every form of illness—fevers, pain, convulsions, wounds, pulled tendons, broken bones, spasms, toothache— even then I would suppress the pure delight that such agonies carry with them," Veronica says of herself, begging Christ to afflict her with other unimaginable punishments.

Women mystics don't write only about torture and self-punishment. Sometimes the sheer joy of living wins out in their writing, sometimes a sense of playfulness. Then eros can crawl back into its den, like a contented little animal who can caress Christ's body without falling prey to the sins of the flesh. "My bridegroom held in one hand a spirited white dove, who played with him and showered him with attention," writes Maria Cecilia Baij (1694–1766), who by the time she was eleven was living among the Cistercians. Two years later she left to become a member of the Benedictine nuns of Montefiascone. She received the stigmata and wrote dialogues and letters: "The dove flew onto his breast, then onto his shoulder. While beating its wings it flew about his neck trying to embrace him, finally nestling its face in his ear. Then it returned to his hand. That's how it would show how happy and joyful it was as it caressed my bridegroom, who for his part was greatly delighted." Can we imagine anything more tender and affectionate, more chaste and at the same time, overtly sensuous?

Maria Cecilia observes that sometimes she was tempted by the devil, who called her "the evil, cursed Cecilia." But she would escape to converse with her celestial spouse, who appeared to her in an imaginary garden. Once she watched as her heart flew out of her bosom and began soaring through the air. Christ, in the form of a handsome young man, "set out to chase that heart," trying to seize it as he followed in pursuit. "Thus did the joust begin: he would toss and turn about to grasp my heart, but my heart would flee and soar away. He asked me, how can a heart fly when it doesn't have wings? And I answered: it is borne into flight through desire alone. He would grasp the heart, but it would escape from him once more. Finally, he managed to catch it with a lasso, and my heart was bound. But while he was squeezing it, it escaped yet again. At the end, exhausted, he drew forth an arrow, gently pierced my heart, and wounded it right in its midst." Could a lovers' duel ever be described with more elegance and delicacy than this?

"With his own mouth he gave me a sweet kiss of holy peace, not once or twice, but many, many times," writes Camilla Battista Varano (1458–1524), who elsewhere discusses her practice of voluntary weeping. This is what she would do: first, once a week, she would reflect on things that were sad, forcing out of herself "a single tear" for the martyrdom of Christ. Then she began doing this every two days, as her weeping became more spontaneous. And then: "And so whereas earlier she had thought on such things and wept once a day, she now began to reflect and weep twice a day, both morning and evening." Varano also wrote *The Mental Sufferings of Christ* and *The Story of My Most Unhappy Happiness*. Sometimes she accuses herself of being a liar and a "most sinful adulteress." But then she listens to the words of Christ, which she finds so sweet that they seem to be made "of honey and sugar, of the tastiest, sweetest manna," and decides that all she wants is to sacrifice herself for him. Camilla laments to a cherub about her unbearable desire for the body of Christ. And the angel responds: "You possess the fire of burning desire. But you're far from the true presence of the body of Christ as well as your own. We angels, however, enjoy this ardent desire in abundance, and in the very presence of him whom we desire. Thus did he command that our great delight would be equal to the greatness of this, our incomprehensible desire."

AUGUST 3. I wonder if Clare ever experienced the joyful moments we've seen with Maria Cecilia Baij, Veronica Giuliani, Brigida Morello, Caterina Paluzzi: those many women mystics who wrote about their lives centuries after Clare. Sometimes their fame extended beyond the walls of their convents. People would come listen to them, and they would become quite well known, as happened with Veronica Giuliani and Angela of Foligno. Others flirted with heretical ideas. The Church's theologians would become quite suspicious of these mystical indulgences. They were particularly intolerant of women's claims that they could communicate directly with God or with Christ, and thus without the mediation of priests. It's not that mystics were openly attacking the authority of the Church; if anything, they could be quite obsequious with respect to papal power. But often their behaviors brushed up against heretical practices, forgetful as they could be of all the prohibitions and rules. They subjected themselves to fasts and corporal punishments that enhanced their sense of themselves as martyrs. They revealed those uncontrollable stigmata to their faithful admirers, they healed the sick, they preached in public—something never accepted by Church law—and they would talk directly to "their Lord."

Many of these women would have ended up on the pyre, accused of sacrilege, were it not for their widespread celebrity and a devout populace who listened to them with adoration and followed them blindly. A few were excellent orators who displayed undeniable charisma. And the Church often found that the easiest and most useful thing to do was to transform them into icons, enclose them within gilded frames, and so render them completely inoffensive. The surest way to silence them was to make them *beatas* or saints. But the Church was careful to make sure that their writings didn't get out, and their written words are still to be found in the drawers of convents, rotting away—for in spite of the command to be silent, these women spoke and wrote, and a great deal, too. Thousands of pages of their words survive—sometimes dictated because they didn't know how to write, sometimes written in their own hand in a Latin or Italian, unsophisticated but beautiful. But the keys to these immense drawers crammed full of texts have been lost.

Listening to her sisters, we gather that Clare was diligent, humble, serene. They don't mention whether she was happy, because it wouldn't have been relevant or interesting to the judges in charge of the canonization trial, during which only the more sobering, traditional qualities of future saints came to light. But given how she conducted herself, how she fostered peace among her sisters, how she worked tirelessly to keep morale high, she must have been capable of joy. In order to oversee a community that was notably expanding after just a few years, in order to convince her young sisters to renounce all their belongings, in order to encourage them to fast for prolonged periods without resorting to psychological ploys or violent force, in order to persuade them that this state of uncertainty about the future was the norm—one could never be sure where the next bite of food would come from: to achieve all this, charisma was essential, along with powerfully strategic intelligence, fierce passion, and considerable peace of mind. I'm sure that Clare knew happiness and could express that to her sisters.

The spirit of the mystic—which derives from the word *mystein* in the Greek, or "keeping a secret"—necessarily interrupts what we think of as classical, rational thought. Logic must be surrendered in order to meditate on the sacred and pursue whatever lies beyond the verisimilar, the comprehensible, things that can be deciphered and explained. The ultimate goal is rapture: a state of ecstasy. A drunkenness of the mind, distanced from all mundane thoughts and free from selfishness. Ecstasy demands the joy of enchantment, the loss of the self.

> May every lover in love with the Lord
> come to the dance and sing of her amour.
> May she come dancing, her heart all inflamed,
> desiring only him, her creator,
> who took her away from earth's dangerous ways.

These are the rhymes of Saint Caterina Vigri (1413–63), who spent much of her life in Bologna. She was born into a well-off Ferrarese family, and her mother taught her how to draw. She painted lovely images of the Madonna, along with her child. She became a Clarissan nun, seeking to reconcile her vow of poverty with her love of and dedication to art. She became famous not for her poetry that sings of the joy of living, nor for her paintings, but because eighteen years after her death, her body was exhumed and discovered to be aromatic and still intact. Not only that: her nails had continued to grow in the tomb, requiring her sisters to trim them back every year. Otherwise they would have become so long that they would have become claws, curling in on themselves. Clement XI made her a saint in 1712.

So much of women's literature has been neglected, hidden, forgotten! I'm sure that one day we'll construct another history of literature in which the writings of women, starting with the mystics, will be placed alongside those of the great authors who are still considered to be the only classics worth reading.

AUGUST 5. Last night I dreamed once again of Clare. That Sicilian Chiara was right when she said that our dreams let us know when we've lost ourselves within the forest of a story. Only when a character is presumptuous enough to enter the mirage that is our dreams does it mean that we've truly welcomed them into the home of our imagination.

The beautiful Clare of Assisi was already stiff on her deathbed. Her waxlike face with its clear skin, her lovely eyelashes resting gently on her pale cheeks, her determined little lips for once relaxed, almost smiling. In my dream, I thought to compare her to an embalmed girl I'd seen many times in the crypt of the Capuchins in Palermo. One simply can't forget this child, so miraculously unblemished that she seems to be sleeping, her head gently resting on a pillow, her soft, weightless hair fanning out about her round skull, her rosy cheeks slightly moist as though she were sweating in her sleep, her perfectly formed little mouth.

They say that when she died, her father was so upset that he swore to find some way to preserve her so that she would still seem to be alive. A doctor, he studied and experimented until he discovered a chemical potion that enabled him to embalm his daughter and keep her close, perfectly preserved, as though she were sleeping. Everyone admired the results and asked him insistently for his secret chemical recipe, but he never revealed it, preferring to carry it with him to the grave rather than have it used by others. And in fact, inside this museum of horror that is the crypt of the Capuchins— where you can see hundreds of corpses with their skin darkened by time, their fleshless faces and teeth protruding from dried lips, their skeletal hands nestled together one on top of the other—this young girl with her rosy, lifelike skin, enclosed within a glass coffin, seems the result of a miracle, a perfect imitation of eternity in the flesh.

In my dream I saw Clare's solid, hardworking hands resting one on top of the other. But I became disconcerted when I realized they were moving—slowly and with difficulty, but in motion. I wanted to help her disentangle those interlaced fingers from the rosary of mother of pearl that kept them bound together. But I couldn't get up. I continued to fix my eyes on those agitated, knowing little hands that finally succeeded in freeing themselves. And then, as though under a spell, they started to dance. A most delicate dance, consisting of slow, stylized movements, reminding me of the ritualized gestures of Japanese actors on the Noh stage. I knew I was dreaming, and I was enjoying this quite extraordinary vision. What a strange visitor she was to my dreamworld—restless, gentle, utterly silent. Even though she was dead, she seemed to want to say something. But what? Those most human and gentle of hands were speaking in an arcane and indecipherable tongue.

By then I'd been inside the convent for far too long, and I started walking through its corridors in my dream without really wanting to. When I once visited San Damiano in Assisi, it was as though my body was following Ariadne's thread as it conducted me through the labyrinth. I could feel the presence of the many women, young and old, who had rested their feet on those stones and those steps; they had prayed, and suffered, and rejoiced in those rooms. I saw on a long table in the refectory their miserable fare, recalling the words of Suor Philippa as she recounted how a peasant had left a loaf of bread at the convent's gate. Seeing it, Clare asked, "Who has left us this loaf of bread?" No one could respond. And she was sad, because "Lady Clare much preferred to receive crumbs for alms, rather than whole loaves."

With the eyes of memory, I saw the Clarissan nuns bowing down to pray at two in the morning, sleepy but obedient; some of them were laboriously coughing, others were blowing their noses into old handkerchiefs they hadn't had time to wash. And here Clare had rested, absorbed in thought. Here she had bent down to gather fresh herbs, here she slept on a sack full of "vine shoots" as the nuns testified, using a stone smoothed by the river for her pillow. Here perhaps she opened a book. Here she had cooked. Here she made the trip that brought her from the kitchen to the courtyard and the courtyard to the kitchen, and from the courtyard to the chapel and from the chapel to the dormitory, and from the dormitory back into the kitchen. How many times would she have gone back and forth during her forty years in the convent? I seemed to hear the pattering of her feet on the icy stones, to see the imprints of plants sweating in August's torrential heat.

I asked if I could meet a Clarissa. They were quite lovely about accommodating my request. They opened the doors to a narrow, unfurnished room, the *parlatorio*. Intent on taking in the smells of the convent—a light scent of disinfectant, of a soup made with chickpeas, of lilies—I wasn't aware that behind the grate of black iron knots a nun had already appeared, her face knowledgeable and serene. She calmly spoke to me in what was clearly an American accent about the history of the convent. While I listened in silence I saw a glimmer of suspicion in her beautiful eyes. And, of course, I was a layperson, visiting a convent of enclosed nuns. What could I possibly write about a woman of whom they knew everything, and I nothing? The other women were invisible, even if I could sense their presence behind the closed doors. Only this nun, with her proud, educated manner of speaking, had been granted permission to talk to me.

Her voice was gentle and clear and carefully controlled. Her face, serene but austere, was framed by the grate. She seemed to be concerned that I would paint a portrait of Clare that wouldn't be very respectful. But that's not my intent. Rather, the more I learn of her, the more I'm seized by admiration for the vital, steely woman who was Clare of Assisi, for her cruel fidelity to herself and to the decisions she made—"And she never could be persuaded either by the pope or by the Bishop of Ostia to receive any possessions. And when the Privilege of Poverty was granted to her, she honored it reverently, guarding it with diligence, careful not to lose it"—for her generosity, for her ability to guide a community without ever having recourse to authority or force, so constant in her faith that to others she could seem celestial and mysterious.

Only when I cited in the course of my conversation a phrase of Suor Balvina's from the canonization process— "and before she became ill, she wanted to go to Morocco"— suggesting that perhaps Clare had wanted to preach in the open air, traveling all the way to Africa to converse with Muslims rather than fight them, as Francis had done when he sought to go unarmed into the enemy camp in Damietta, Egypt, to talk to the sultan Al-Malik al-Kamil—only then did the nun gently contradict me. No, she said, Clare wanted to go to Morocco simply to become a martyr, not to preach or to meet people from another culture. Clare did not wish to be anywhere else. She chose to remain enclosed in her convent for her entire life. If she had left, it would have been only to confront her execution.

Back in my dream, I asked myself if Clare really had sought martyrdom. And the answer came back that yes, she felt it was the only path worthy of meriting Christ's love, a Christ who had been a martyr himself. And Christ, I continued to ask myself in my dream, had he chosen of his own free will to be crucified? Had he sought out pain, torture, death? The answer was yes, that's what he chose. And if instead he had sought the opposite, to liberate himself from those nails of the cross and escape his martyrdom, could he have done so? Again the answer was yes, he could have, but he didn't want to, because his martyrdom served the purpose of redeeming all humankind. Is this why true Christians thirst for martyrdom? The answer was always yes. But my stupid, rationalizing brain did not give up, and continued to ask: Is it really possible that there is redemption only in pain? Then what is joy about? Only sin and disobedience? Doesn't Francis speak of a pure love for all creatures in his *laude*, his poems of praise? Don't we find happiness and joy in his words?

AUGUST 7. My back was aching all night long. I woke up, sat leaning against the wall, and said to myself: look, if Clare were here and she rested her hand on my back, the pain would disappear like magic. This means you're entering into her story, a voice said, smiling, somewhere within my drowsy brain. I held in my hand the precious book of testimonies for her canonization and set out to look for references to miracles Clare had performed on others' infirm bodies. Balvina, Clare's niece who entered the convent in the summer of 1212, just a few months after her aunt, testifies that "one night she was very distressed by a sharp pain in her hip and began to ache and complain. And Lady Clare asked what was wrong. Then the witness told her about her suffering, and the mother threw herself onto her hip, where it was hurting. Then she covered the witness's hip with the veil she had been wearing, and instantly all the pain vanished."

The judge asked Balvina when this happened, and she answered, "twelve or more years ago." So Clare herself was already sick and was no longer leaving her bed. Yet the desire to help free Balvina from pain moved her to rise up from her sickbed and drag herself—can we use the word "drag" if it's true that Clare could move only with the help of two nuns?—to her niece and "throw herself" across her hip. Then Clare covered her hip with the very cloth that she herself wore on her head (then they all slept wearing their habits? Or was it because it was so cold and because she lay so close to the soil that Clare covered her head even at night?), and the pain vanished. There is something impetuous, something impassioned about the way she embraced her niece's infected hip. As if she wanted to engage her entire body in healing someone else, even though she was so ill herself.

Another time, "the witness for the aforementioned Saint Clare was liberated from a continuous fever, and from an abscess in her right breast, from which the other sisters thought she was about to die. And this had happened twenty years ago. Asked how long she had the fever, she answered, 'three days.'" It's clear from these testimonials that Balvina was in poor health. Twice Clare intervened when others thought the nun was going to die. Twice Clare healed her niece, making the sign of the cross over the body of the sick woman. The nuns thanked her each time, but she wouldn't accept their thanks. It was not she who healed them, but Christ, her celestial bridegroom.

The miracles of Saint Clare are moving for their simple quotidian nature. Like that of the stray cat: "It was also said by this witness that once when Clare couldn't get out of bed because of her infirmity, she asked that a piece of linen be brought to her, but there was no one to bring it. Suddenly one of the convent cats began to yank and pull at the cloth, so as to bring it to her as best she could." So even the cats loved her, and they helped her when they could. What would such an intelligent creature have been named? And did it have permission to jump onto the sick woman's lap to purr?

We don't know about other animals, but we do know about this affectionate cat. In the convent of San Damiano there once roamed a cat, nameless but incredibly smart, who understood Clare's words so well that she grasped her request for a table linen and dragged it over to her bed. Was it a miracle, or only the intuition of an affectionate animal? It's not important. It's nice to know that despite her constant pain and enforced immobility, Clare had a loving relationship with a cat. Were there other cats in the convent? Did they have names? Were there dogs, goats, geese, chickens? It's likely that since the nuns refused all property, even possessing a domestic animal would be considered a sin. That's how Francis saw it. Especially hens that laid eggs, I imagine, or goats that gave milk. Cats were admissible, on the other hand, because they had no use other than catching mice. Is this why cats frequented San Damiano? Were there mice in the convent?

I would think so. Tiny country mice that got into everything, leaving their droppings in pans and in the laundry, as they still do today. They're the most difficult creatures to get rid of because they climb in through a crack under the door or nest in a ball of cotton that's lying forgotten under a stair. It's happened to me, such as when I found one in the refrigerator of my country house. It came in through an aeration vent, grabbed some food in a hurry before it could freeze, and went right back into the tube. Another time as I was putting on a jacket that had been hanging in the entryway, two mice jumped out of the pockets, one from the left and the other from the right, scared out of their wits. How could I have permitted myself to disturb their refuge after a month's absence?

Who knows if Clare was afraid of mice, as is the case with so many women? A fear that probably goes back for centuries, since mice carried the plague. But as I think about it, I'm convinced that Clare didn't fear these tiny creatures of God that scurried around the convent. Perhaps the cat would capture them. Clare certainly wouldn't have killed them herself. Generous as she was toward all creatures and attentive to their needs, she would have had respect even for mice, who can't be blamed for being mice and for being hungry. Just like fleas or mosquitoes or lice or ticks—it's not their fault. But we do know that Clare valued cleanliness, and that when one nun had lice it's likely that Clare rubbed a paste made of tar and oil into her hair to get rid of the parasites. Up to what point is it mandated that we must co-exist with God's smallest creatures? I would have liked to ask this of Saint Francis. Isn't an ant also God's creature? But if an army of ants invades the kitchen in search of food and assaults a piece of bread that's soaking in a few drops of olive oil on a plate, and that's the only meal of the day, what is one to do?

The relationship between Christians and animals has always been a mystery to me. Sometimes it appears to be one of great tenderness, sometimes it's virtually nonexistent. It's true that Francis loved animals. One grasps this from his beautiful *laude*, even if he doesn't mention animals specifically. The love that he felt for the sun, the moon, and the stars: surely it doesn't exclude forests, trees, and animals, creatures of the Lord. There's the episode of the wolf of Gubbio, which many historians have wanted to interpret figuratively as an encounter with the enemy. But wolves never travel alone. They go about in packs, and attack only when they know they're stronger and more numerous than their prey, whom they surround and drive into a corner. There's political significance too, in the most elevated sense of the word, in the story of the wolf of Gubbio. Legend has it that Francis spoke to the wolf and proposed a truce. He didn't change his nature or transform him into a lamb by uttering a few magic words, which as a saint he could easily have done. Francis valued reality and sought to act in order to bring about peace, not war. He promoted justice, not handouts.

Francis spoke with this fierce wolf and convinced him that he should no longer attack sheep and men. In exchange, he guaranteed that every day the citizens of Gubbio would provide him with food. It was a pact, almost a contract. The extraordinary thing is that Francis thought that one might be able to arrange such a contract with an animal, considering it worthy of respect. This is what is so original and new about his way of thinking. I like to think of it not as a gift conferred by a benevolent master on his servant, or an act of almsgiving, but as a treaty between equals.

Thus the revolutionary nature of the exchange with the wolf. Above all, Francis believed in the equality of all living beings. He put his faith in dialogue, in example, in bargaining, in tolerance: in sum, in true politics, the kind that looks for a way to enable people of diverse thinking, backgrounds, ideas, political sensibilities, even diverse species, to live together through trust, reasoning, and mutual understanding. For those who believe only in the law of force and destroying one's enemies, all this could only irritate, like smoke in one's eyes. A great many people, in fact, felt that Francis and Clare were blowing smoke into their eyes.

"When [Francis] was approaching Bevagna, he came upon a place where a large flock of birds of various kinds had gathered," Bonaventure of Bagnoregio recounts in his

Legenda Maior. As he preached to the birds, "they began to stretch their necks, spread their wings, open their beaks and look at him. He passed through their midst with amazing fervor of spirit, touching them with his tunic . . . and his companions waiting along the way noticed all these things." Giotto gave us a lovely image of the saint already aging, turning toward these winged creatures the same gentle disposition he used when he spoke to human beings.

I'd like to imagine that Clare had this same kind of affectionate and indulgent relationship with the cat. At times, however, cats bring embarrassing gifts, as when they deliver to a beloved human their mangled prey. How would our infirm Clare, her hands eternally busied with embroidery, have reacted to the cruel gift of a mouse mauled by a cat and left at her feet? I think Clare would have chided the cat for its ferocity, but with a sweet voice, and then she would have given it a caress because she well knew this was the nature of felines, and that the bloodied prey was a gift given with love.

AUGUST 8. Clare's temperament comes through so forcefully in her sisters' testimonials that you feel as though you know her. She did not enjoy being in charge even though she was the abbess or governess of the convent. She did not order people around, she did not prescribe, she did not reprimand. She suggested and persuaded, like an older, maternal sister who is trying above all to protect her youngest sibling: "If at times the previously mentioned Madonna Clare saw some of her sisters suffering from some temptation or tribulation, that lady would secretly call them to her side, and weeping she would console them, sometimes even throwing herself at their feet." We've already heard this from other witnesses. When one of the flock was overtaken by discomfort, rage, or sadness, she was rebelling against and disobeying the rules of the community. Clare would take her aside and press her to think about what she was doing. If that didn't manage to convince her, she would burst into tears, throwing herself at the feet of the woman who had strayed. And the prodigal certainly couldn't resist. How does one argue with an abbess who has thrown herself onto the floor in front of you, tearfully pleading with you to make amends?

"Such was her mildness and sweetness in admonishing her sisters, and in the other good and holy things that she did, that one's tongue cannot possibly tell of all that was in Lady Clare." We can gather from this and other episodes that Clare had an anxious and emotional temperament, though she never lost control over herself. She embraced Balvina's hip to cure her, she genuflected on the ground before an errant nun to convince her to repent. Similarly, she prostrated herself in tears before the Saracens, begging Christ to send them away. And the Saracens complied, and immediately took off.

Reassured, Clare is helped to her feet by Illuminata di Pisa and another nun who died before the canonization process. With her gracious sense of pride, Clare made all the nuns promise never to tell anyone what had happened. But she was especially stern with the two nuns who had carried her from her bed into the courtyard: "Mother Clare called them both and commanded them that while she was alive, they would say nothing to anyone." But the news circulated nonetheless, and soon the entire city knew that the Saracens had been chased out of the convent of San Damiano by Mother Clare.

Benvenuta of Perugia recounts the scene in clear, flowing words. "Once, during the war with Assisi, certain Saracens mounted up on the wall, and climbed down into the cloister of San Damiano. The aforementioned holy mother, Madonna Chiara, who by then was gravely ill, got up from her bed and had the sisters called together, comforting them so they would not be fearful. And when her prayer was finished, the Lord liberated the convent and the sisters from the enemy. And those Saracens who had entered departed." Historians have sought for some logical explanation for this sudden change of heart. Had an order arrived from Frederick II, who knew of the convent's fame? Invading San Damiano and any subsequent violence done to the nuns would certainly have cost him more than he would have gained by taking part of the city. Or perhaps once they realized how desperately poor the convent was and that there was nothing precious to steal, the Saracens went off to find booty elsewhere. These are historical suppositions. To believe in miracles, one must have a pure heart and the conviction that mystery overwhelms the logic of events.

AUGUST 9. I had an incredibly vivid dream: dressed in a torn and dirty sackcloth, Clare was walking up and down in the little courtyard of San Damiano, carrying an infant in her arms, its naked body emaciated and thin. Clare's eyes were so intense, so bright, so happy, that I started smiling in my sleep. Clare loved children. Did she regret not having any? All the witnesses speak of her tender and generous love for them. Often sick babies were brought to the convent so that Clare would cure them. She never once refused, even if she hated being thought of as a healer. There was something presumptuous about that miraculous power they attributed to her, and she did not appreciate being hailed as a "phenomenon." Above all, the public's admiration and naïve gratitude embarrassed her. Time and time again she humbly insisted that she was not the one who healed, but Christ. Her earthly flesh had no power to change or modify nature. How could her diseased body perform miracles if she couldn't even stand up on her own two feet? A holy fluid ran through her veins, accompanied by the generosity of divine grace: that's what made her hands so warm and reassuring, her breath so precious.

"She also said that another nun, Suor Cecilia, had a nasty cough, so severe that as soon as she started to eat, it seemed as though she was going to drown. So the aforementioned holy mother, on the *sexta feria*—a Friday—gave her a piece of focaccia to eat, and she took it with great trepidation, but because it was a command from her holy mother, she ate it. And from then on she was no longer sick." A piece of focaccia treated like a host, containing the body of Christ. Is this the meaning of the miracle? "Suor Amata of Messer Martino of Cocorano, nun of the monastery of San Damiano, so swears." That's the oath the witnesses would take when standing before the judges sent to Assisi by the pope.

Even though she knew that Suor Cecilia couldn't eat anything because she started to suffocate no matter what she put into her mouth, Clare suggested that she gulp down the piece of bread that she handed her with her delicate fingers. Cecilia feared she would choke, and she looked at the bread nervously. But then she obeyed, not only because it was her abbess who ordered her to do so, but because this was a special abbess; they knew she could perform miracles, and as doubtful as she may have felt, she also thought she could trust her. In fact, as the witness says, she was immediately cured of that cursed cough. But Clare asked her too not to let anyone know, because she didn't want others to hear of these little miracles.

The word got out and spread so far that on some days there was a line outside the gate in front of the convent. Men, women, and especially children sought that healing hand: "She also said that a baby from Perugia had a film covering its entire eye, and they took him to Saint Clare, who touched the boy's eye and made the sign of the cross. And then she said, 'Take him to my mother, Suor Ortolana, so she can make the sign of the cross over him.' Once that was done, the boy was cured. Thus Saint Clare said that her mother had liberated him, while her mother insisted that it was Lady Clare, her daughter, who had healed him. Thus each of them gave this honor to the other."

The judge asked the witness if she had seen the stain disappear in person. Suor Amata answered that she had seen the boy with the infected eye when they brought him to the convent, but she didn't see him after he was healed, because the child was taken away in great haste. But she had heard that he was cured. And this time, too, Clare asked that her sisters remain silent.

This testimony about Ortolana might seem odd insofar as it involves Clare's mother in an act of healing. What did Clare mean by this gesture? Did she want to demonstrate that anyone who dedicated herself to prayer and to the love of Christ could heal a sick child? Or did she want to show that because Ortolana was her mother, she shared Clare's miraculous powers? Or that the body of the daughter had inherited her mother's traits and so if she, Clare, was able to heal others, she owed it to Ortolana, who was the first to have been given such a gift?

One can imagine that Clare may have sought to protect herself from the demands of her fellow citizens by asking her mother to cure the sick who were begging to be cured. Such fame could turn out to be dangerous. What if the child on whom you'd laid your hand and made the sign of the cross should die? What if the blemish in a little boy's eye grew larger instead of going away, and the boy lost his sight? Her reputation could be damaged. Still, people continued to run to her. And even though she was reluctant, Clare did not hold back. She knew that they needed her. And why not at least try? Her faith in Christ was such that she was able to convey it to whoever approached her. And faith and hope, we know, are contagious; they can relieve any form of suffering.

In my dream, Clare was wearing a Franciscan habit, made of that coarse wool the nuns called "lasso" in the testimonials, a word from the Umbrian dialect for muslin. She had another piece of white cloth draped over her hair and around her neck, from which a rebellious curl had escaped. As I watched her, I said to myself that she hadn't put her head covering or *camauro* on very carefully—not because she was vain, but from absentmindedness. I've noticed that in some paintings and drawings, Clare is wearing this *camauro*, a kind of white stocking you put on your head, which leaves the face uncovered while concealing the neck and hair. Above that she has on a veil. In other images she wears no such head cover. Instead, Clare and the women of San Damiano are depicted in long, brown tunics cut in an oval shape around the neck, which remains exposed. Over their heads are black veils that must have been lined in white, because a light-colored material can be seen in the cuffs and folds of the fabric.

I was arguing with myself in my dream. I was saying that you can see that Clare's illness sometimes prevented her from putting in the effort she needed to look neat and clean, despite her poverty. That curl jumped out only by chance. But no, I'm stupid: the nuns would have shaved their heads. I went back and forth with myself in my dream. But hair grows back, and you can't possibly shave it every day as though it were a beard. When days go by without shaving your head, hair will start growing back on a bald cranium. But did the nuns shave themselves, or assist one another? All right, enough of these irreverent thoughts. No one has ever posed these problems with respect to a saint. Yet such issues were real, the stuff of daily life, and they had nothing to do with prayer and meditation. A writer is nurtured on these precious details that make up the weave of time itself, the daily fabric of which one's hours are made. Sometimes they're insignificant details, but when they're lined up, they help construct a place, tell a story.

Still dreaming, I gazed at Clare more carefully. And I understood: in that instant, she wasn't thinking about her *camauro* or a veil put on hastily, about a curl that escaped her control, about her freezing feet. Like her thoughts, her gaze was wholly absorbed in the child she held in her arms, who slept so intently that nothing could disturb him. His tiny fists were closed, and his head reclined on her bosom almost as though he had just finished nursing, his chubby feet in the air. And Clare was gently cradling him, swaying him delicately in her arms. Her gaze was full of the moon and the stars, or so I thought in my dream, even citing to myself a line of classical poetry without realizing it. A Madonna with child. A virgin Mother, her baby born in her womb through the intervention of the Holy Spirit.

My dream was probably influenced from having read right before I went to bed a lengthy interview with the pastor of the monastic community of Bose, Father Enzo Bianchi, published in the newspaper *La Repubblica* on July 28. He mentioned something I'd never heard a monk say, that he was nostalgic for a son. I asked myself whether paternal sentiments could be as strong and meaningful as maternal feelings, which we attribute only to women. If the prior of Bose, a chaste and pious man, dedicated to preaching and praising God, says without fear of scandal and with surprising candor that he would like to have had a son, it means that such a desire is universal and that it's not offset by giving one's body over to God. It's not a sin that violates chastity.

A man must have sex to produce a child, and unless he has recourse to a prostitute, he must love a woman. It's possible that the pastor of Bose wanted to suggest that it wouldn't be such a bad or dangerous thing if men dedicated to the church were to get married. Or he may have been saying that love is never wrong as long as it does not seek harm to another. In any case, Protestant priests marry and have children, and they love their families just as they love Christ. It doesn't mean they're worse priests than the chaste Catholics. The pastor of Bose makes a subtle distinction, moreover, between priests who depend strictly on the ecclesiastical hierarchy, and monks whose relationship to God is more direct, who respect the Church's authority but aren't enslaved to it. Weren't these exactly the kinds of things Saint Clare was thinking and saying?

Recently I read a book that's usually thought to have been written just for children: *Pinocchio*. But it really needs to be read by adults. In addition to Carlo Collodi's marvelous use of the Tuscan tongue and his concise and forthright style, the book's extraordinary originality consists in the way it intelligently explores the intense and often repressed longing of a man to be a father. Geppetto is all alone, old, and poor. The only way for him to have a son is to make one. And so he does, carving a boy from a piece of wood. But he does it so well that as soon as he finishes adjusting its feet, the marionette gets up and starts to run around. And Geppetto runs after him, with the constancy, patience, delight, love, and dedication of a father to a son who is wanted and loved. In the end, it will be his love that transforms the marionette into a real boy—the father's love, more than the son's repentance. A love so tender and generous that it can breach the gulf between animate and inanimate objects.

It's striking that a book so centered on paternal love doesn't provoke hatred or scorn for mothers. The mother is simply absent in *Pinocchio*. But not because she is considered unworthy or insignificant, and not even because the man is overcome by fantasies of omnipotence, but probably because, as so often happened in those days, she died in childbirth. What mattered to Collodi at that moment was the hidden and oft-suppressed sentiment of paternity that lodges in the heart of every man. A paternity that is attentive, sweet, willing to make sacrifices, timidly apprehensive, generous, patient, tolerant, and altruistic—all qualities generally delegated to women, as if a man couldn't, and shouldn't, harbor tender and delicate feelings in his manly heart. As if kindness were a vice, a way of giving in to the emotional world of the feminine, far from the myth of a virility based wholly on control, detachment, freedom from sentimentality, brute conquest.

The only woman who shows up in Collodi's story is dead. But she's pretty and kind in death. And she's also ironic. She is the fairy with blue hair. When he goes to knock at her door, and "it became clear to him that knocking served no purpose, out of desperation he began to kick the door and bang his head against it. And then a lovely Little Girl appeared at the window. Her hair was blue and her face as white as a waxen image. Her eyes were closed and her hands were crossed on her chest, and without the slightest movement of her lips she said, in a faint voice that seemed to come from the world beyond: 'There is no one in this house. They are all dead.' 'Well then,' shouted Pinocchio, crying and pleading with her, 'you open up for me.' 'But I am dead, too.' 'Dead? But then whatever are you doing up there at the window?' 'I'm waiting for the casket to come and take me away.' As soon as she said this, the Little Girl disappeared, and the window closed again without making a sound." In Collodi's marvelous book, there's not the slightest hint of wanting to demonize mothers, even as it dwells on paternal love.

During the canonization proceedings for Clare, Suor Francesca testified that "a young boy, son of Messer Johanni de Assisi, had a fever and the scrofula, and this saint made the sign of the cross over him and touched him, and he was freed." Clare did not limit herself to making the sign of the cross on his forehead: she touched him as well. In other words, she took him in her arms, rested a hand on the nape of his neck, and gazed into his feverish eyes, possibly realizing that the child had a swollen belly and scrofula all over his body. Today we would say that he had measles, or scarlet fever. But Clare wasn't afraid of these diseases. Illness was a sign of divine will. The Lord sent poor health for reasons best known only to himself, secret and inscrutable as he was. Hadn't she been ill for many years? If sickness were a sign of divine punishment, of what fault could she be accused, she who wore a scratchy hair shirt beneath her garments, who fasted so severely that Francis had to urge her to eat more, who prayed day and night, who slept on a sack filled with vine shoots and used a stone for a pillow: of what could she possibly be to blame?

This was a silly and disrespectful question, I realized in the course of my dream. As if one could challenge decisions made in heaven! It's arrogant and useless to talk about God's will. He has his own mysterious reasons that we know nothing about, his motives too profound and indecipherable to ever be explained. There's nothing more pathetic than human reason confounded before the mystery of the divine, or so Clare seems to tell us in those few portraits that survive, with her perfectly oval face, her eyes the shape of almonds, her little mouth perennially closed, her gaze humble and absorbed in thought. It's ridiculous to argue in front of the unknowable immensity that is the mind of God. Why come up with useless questions?

Who knows if our Clare held that *mammolo*—that little boy—in her arms! Who knows if she cradled him as I imagined her doing during last night's dream? Who knows if Clare, who was so hard on herself—"she never wanted to pardon her own body," in the words of Suor Cecilia—who knows if for just that once, she allowed her confined, constrained, mortified, tormented body to experience joy? A joy that was calm, sensual, innocent, and affectionate in the company of this little child—a *mammolo* whose fever she tried to cure with all the forces she could summon up within herself?

"At [his] beauty the sun and the moon marvel," Clare wrote to Agnes of Bohemia in the third letter, speaking of the Christ child. His "rewards and their uniqueness and grandeur have no limits; I am speaking of Him, the Son of the Most High, whom the Virgin brought to birth and remained a virgin after His birth. May you cling to His most sweet mother who gave birth to a Son Whom the heavens could not contain, and yet she carried Him in the little cloister of her holy womb and held Him on her virginal lap." What an original and beautiful metaphor: the cloister of her womb, a comparison that would occur only to a nun, but put with such delicacy and force.

"This witness also said that once on a day in May, she saw sitting on the lap of Lady Clare just in front of her bosom a beautiful *mammolo*, so beautiful that one can't begin to express it. And this very witness, upon seeing that *mammolo*, began to feel an indescribable sweetness. And without doubt, she believed that the child was the Son of God." These may have been the words that inspired my dream. The child was indeed lovely, as we see in certain Madonnas by Leonardo. A fat and peaceful baby boy, his eyes piercing and clear, his curly baby hair framing a halo about his round face, with chubby little arms and fat little feet strong enough to propel themselves up into the air like tiny flowers made of flesh.

Still dreaming, I started thinking, what a strange thing to hold one's own baby husband in one's arms! A truly surprising contradiction, I said to myself: bridegroom and son at the same time. But in the kingdom of faith, there is no such thing as time, and everything is possible. In a time that has no time, a son grows up quickly to become a man, and then a husband, while his mother remains young, shrouded in her blue robes, transforming herself into his bride. This is flight in two directions at once, with two different rhythms, swift and full of desire, and its result is this encounter, singularly miraculous!

AUGUST 10. I awoke with these words on my lips: time does not exist. Even when the clock was right there on my nightstand to tell me that it does, and that it's made up of hours, minutes, and seconds. But it was the clock itself that suggested to me the idea that time isn't real. Otherwise, why would we be so insistent about how to divide time up, so precise about its metrics? All we have to do is compare just for a moment our own sense of time with that of the universe to realize that something's not right. Here we talk of counting and saving minutes; there one speaks of millions and billions of light years, and we have no idea if those years are moving or motionless—and if they go backward or forward, toward an expansion of the cosmos that will finish in a colossal explosion, or toward a contraction that will reduce the entire galaxy to the size of a tennis ball: a pure concentration of light. Who knows? And in order to convince ourselves of time's passing—the only thing that we're aware of since we feel it on our very skin—we invented that silly object, awkward but extremely useful and at its heart, even poetic: the clock. A pathetic and altogether human scheme for survival.

But with respect to the universe: who's to say that our sense of time doesn't correspond to the duration of the life of an insect that lives and dies in a single day? Even an insect divvies up, rearranges, enlarges his tiny vital space to reduce it to the measure of his brain, and why shouldn't that single day feel as long to him as a human life span to us? So it is that we count, parse, measure out our day, its hours and minutes, reducing this mysterious duration to the measure of man so we can render it comprehensible and controllable. And even lovable. Otherwise, how would we manage to live? Only faith in an immutable and eternal God, friend to mankind, can reassure anxious souls.

When Clare was alive, time was both more flexible and more rigid than it is today. It was punctuated by church bells, by the sweep the sun made around the earth (as the Church then maintained). Time had the rhythm of meals, the practice of prayer: Matins, Nones, Compline. How did Clare conquer the monotony of time in that tiny prison space of San Damiano where she was confined? Did she invent poetic, mental clocks to which to entrust her daily survival? Repetition anesthetizes. It can also kill.

A clever short story by Luigi Pirandello, "The Train Has Whistled," tells of a clerk who's half mad, who every day repeats the same gestures, fills out the same forms, takes the same route from his house to the office and from the office back home. Only once does he raise his head to notice something, when he hears the whistle of a train. That same train has always gone by and it has always blown its whistle, though he'd never noticed. But one day he hears it and looks up from his papers. Although he doesn't know it, it will also be his last day in the real world. But he feels that something is about to change, suddenly aware that there has never been any difference for him between one day or a hundred days. When gestures are endlessly repeated in an identical way, they become invisible and disappear, eventually resembling an eternity that has no meaning.

Did embroidering corporals allow Clare to salvage an understanding of time that she could cope with? Or to her brave and orderly mind, did time itself take the form of a becoming that flew like an arrow toward its splendid goal: her encounter with her spouse, her entrance into some fixed, stable eternity of the senses? "The said witness also mentioned that Lady Clare was so absorbed in contemplation on the day of Good Friday, when she would reflect on the passion of our Lord, she would seem almost numb for the entire day and most of the following night." Was this how Clare lived out her sense of time? Escaping from her monotonous seclusion by way of a sickly body that had become so sensitive that she had to abandon her burdensome flesh on a sack of straw in order to enter into a distant, feverish passion of Christian love, her senses awakened? Thanks to mental levitation and the straining of her fantasy, had she become capable of living elsewhere, bypassing centuries to arrive in the blink of an eye before the body of Jesus?

So absorbed was she in contemplation, Suor Philippa testifies, that she would become utterly motionless, as though she were caught up in a trance. Where was Clare's imagination while her laborious hands twisted themselves around on her lap, if not at the gate of the great Roman city of Jerusalem on the day of the passion? Was she not there with Christ under the raging sun of a merciless Palestine, feeling on her own skin the scourge of the whip with which a Roman soldier prodded her to stay on the path, despite the flies eating away at her face, the blood pouring from her temples into her eyes, her bare feet stumbling over the stones, the cries of the feverish crowd? And while the workers were digging a hole in the earth in which they would bury the base of the cross, was she not staring, dismayed, at the wood on which she would soon be immobilized? And wasn't she barely containing herself from crying out when she felt the sharp point of the nail penetrate the naked palm of her hand?

The nuns would watch her, in wonder. Clare had a stunning capacity for sacrifice. How did she manage to endure such discomfort and painful paralysis, lying on her repellent sack of straw, racked by disease? Suor Benvenuta of Perugia tells us that "in the place where this Madonna Clare used to go pray, she saw above her a great splendor of light, so much light that she thought the room was on fire." A flame that surrounded her as though she was being burned alive. And Clare burned. She burned from religious passion and the fever of excitement, she burned with unrequited love. Was that why her legs didn't move? Often the sisters would see her suddenly stiffen up in the middle of her chores, her body so rigid she seemed to be dead. Those were the moments when her mind set off on its journey, abandoning her inert limbs on that mattress of straw that she knew only too well, so she could go off and visit faraway landscapes and places unknown yet thoroughly dear to her spirit.

Was there such a thing as the mystical practice of martyrdom during those long centuries of religious totalitarianism?

Absolute poverty, uncertainty about the future, surrendering to illness and deprivation: wasn't it all a form of religious mysticism heedless of any authority that was not divine? The mystic seeks to render a nameless and unknown God visible, by having him descend from heaven so that he might receive a name and become flesh. Mystics insist that religion be separate from politics. They are often prophets, sought out by the crowd for their gifts. Savonarola was condemned unjustly, or so said those mystics who often cited his words and ideas about prioritizing the individual and one's conscience over dogma. For mystics, God is a sexed body. But it's a body that's been humiliated, wounded, beaten, nailed to the cross. Mystics want to retrace his steps to Calvary.

Excluded from liturgical rites, prevented from having direct access to Sacred Scripture, and incited by the Latin language of the breviary, women mystics sought refuge in a direct relationship with God—one that extended from their tiny cells to the highest reaches of heaven, from their beds of suffering to a place of secret repose with a Father (but often, also a Mother) of love. If the Church was going to imprison them and deprive them of speech, they would give themselves the right to preach, even if privately within the convent. This didn't keep them from becoming famous, adored by a populace who rushed to hear them. What was their secret to avoid being reported to the authorities of the Inquisition? It was to respect power and hierarchy, but only on the surface—and to dwell at a remove from those hierarchies, engaging in an ongoing battle between rules and autonomy.

AUGUST 22. Francis is extremely ill. He's suffering from an eye disease that has left him almost completely blind. Any light hurts his pupils. He's never been the picture of health, but all of his traveling, especially to Africa, has left him debilitated.

He lives in darkness, in a hovel infested by mice. Clare comes to learn of his illness. Might she have considered sending him a kitten to rid him of the mice? No chronicle says anything about it. But Francis has the marvelous capacity to turn evil into good, pain into serenity. In fact, at exactly the height of this painful eye disease and the malarial fevers that so weakened him, he composed one of the most beautiful poems in the Italian language:

Most high, omnipotent, good Lord,
praise, glory and honor are yours, and every blessing;
to you alone, most high, do they all belong,
and no man is worthy to utter your name.
My Lord, praise be to you and all your creatures,
especially sir brother sun,
who is the day, and brings us his light.
And he is lovely and radiant with great splendor:
O Highest one, he bears your likeness.
My Lord, praise be to you for sister Moon and all the stars:
you formed them in heaven, and they are clear, and
    precious, and lovely.
My Lord, praise be to you for brother wind,
for the air and clouds, for calm and every kind of weather,
through which you nurture all your creatures.
My Lord, praise be to you for sister water,
who is so useful and humble and precious and chaste.
My Lord, praise be to you for brother fire,
who brightens our night,
and he is handsome and happy and robust and strong.
My Lord, praise be to you for our sister, mother earth,
who sustains us and governs us,
and produces every kind of fruit, and colorful flower
    and herb.

My Lord, praise be to you for those who pardon out of love
    for you,
and suffer infirmities and tribulations.
Blessed are they who maintain the peace,
for they will be crowned, Highest one, by you.
My Lord, praise be to you for our sister, bodily death,
whom no living being can escape:
woe to those who die in mortal sin;
blessed are those whom death will find in your
    holiest graces,
for this second death will bring them no harm.
Praise and bless and thank my Lord,
And serve him with great humility.

It's hard to imagine a mind more naturally disposed to happiness. A happiness that must be created, beginning with words. A happiness that consists more than anything else in respecting and honoring what lives outside of us, what is even against us, including death itself. Francis's prayer embodies an entire philosophy of the world, a giving of oneself that becomes so expansive and radiant that it communicates merriment—the highest form of mirth, tied to the sacredness of creation. A merriment that links everything together through the sheer joy of existence: whether it's celebrating animals or trees, the heavens or human beings. Entities that aren't separate from one another, that aren't intent on devouring one another, but united in a maternal embrace and bathed in the scent of primordial milk. I'm glad I learned this poem in school when I was young. Even when it seems like there's nothing in there, my memory still carries on its surface the traces of these words that have marked me forever in their beauty and largesse.

Some manuscripts indicate that the text was furnished with a musical accompaniment of which unfortunately not a hint remains. It seems that Francis sang the words himself, along with his brothers in the church of Santa Maria degli Angeli. Who knows if Clare had any way of listening to him sing? She would often send him messages asking him to come say a few words to her sisters. She begged him to visit her poor little ones, her "little plants" as she once called them. But he didn't show up. As though he feared exposing himself to too much tenderness.

The only time he agreed to visit the convent of San Damiano, which he himself helped to build, he surprised the sisters by his silence. They were expecting a prophecy, a story, some words of consolation. And instead he arrived with his head down, pensive. He took a handful of ashes from the hearth and spread them out into a circle. He crouched in its midst, then covered his head with those very ashes, reciting a *miserere*. Then he got up and left without saying a word.

The sisters were stunned, no doubt somewhat mortified by behavior that seemed almost contemptuous. But Francis was not being contemptuous. He was inclined to use gestures. When he thought words weren't necessary, he would express himself through what could be called a mystical sense of theatricality, dignified and intense, just as though he were in a sacred play. He's someone who once took his clothes off in public—a powerful gesture, designed to reveal himself as naked and fragile before his father and the authorities of Assisi. And the scene with the ashes should certainly be interpreted in the same way. Here too we're confronted with a ceremony shrouded in solemnity and theatricality. As though he is saying, I don't need words with you sisters, you know everything about me and I know everything about you.

We share the same ideas, we have the same feelings. I want only to confirm right here, with you, our practice of humbling ourselves before God. Ashes we were once and to ashes we shall return. I have nothing else to say.

And in any case, he had already uttered his words of wisdom to the poor sisters. They would be included in the Rule of Clare or *Forma Vitae*, as she writes in chapter 6: "I, brother Francis, the little one, wish to follow the life and the poverty of our most high Lord, Jesus Christ, and of his most holy Mother, and to persevere in this until the end; and I ask and counsel you, my ladies, to live always in this most holy life and in poverty. And keep most careful watch that you never depart from this by reason of the teaching or advice of another."

There's something touching about the way he refers to himself as little Francis. A minor friar, the least of the least, he who could have been a knight! He could have traveled the world wearing the fanciest and most expensive of clothes. He preferred to turn himself into a poor, insignificant friar. One of the oldest and most authentic portraits of Francis, according to scholars, is that of Cimabue. He is skinny, certainly not very charming: his mouth is a trifle crooked, his ears too large, his eyes wide, luminous, damp. A magnetic gaze which was no doubt accompanied by a persuasive and charismatic voice.

"Since by divine inspiration you have made yourselves daughters and handmaidens of the most high King, the heavenly Father, and have taken the Holy Spirit as your spouse, choosing to live according to the perfection of the holy Gospel, I resolve and promise for myself and for my brothers always to have that same loving care and special solicitude for you as [I have] for them." The Friars Minor lived very close to the Poor Sisters, going out every day to beg and bring bread, oil, milk, and vegetables to the convent.

Clare responds in her own Rule to Francis's words: "Just as I, together with my sisters, have been ever solicitous to safeguard the holy poverty which we have promised the Lord and the beloved Francis, so too, the abbesses who shall succeed me in office and all the sisters are bound to observe it inviolably to the end: that is to say, they are not to receive or to hold onto any possessions or property [acquired] through an intermediary, or even anything that might be reasonably called property, except as much land as necessity requires for the integrity and the proper seclusion of the monastery; and this land is not to be cultivated except as a garden for the needs of the sisters."

The rule for which she had worn herself out in the hopes of obtaining papal approval arrived, a precious gift, two days before her death. From the sisters' accounts, we learn that she humbly kissed it with tears in her eyes, holding it next to her heart. "The sisters shall not acquire anything as their own, neither a house nor a place nor anything at all," Clare obsessively repeats. "As pilgrims and strangers in this world who serve the Lord in poverty and humility, let them send confidently for alms. Nor should they feel ashamed, since the Lord made Himself poor for us in this world. This is that summit of highest poverty which has established you, my dearest sisters, as heirs and queens of the kingdom of heaven; it has made you poor in the things [of this world] but has exalted you in virtue."

Pilgrims and strangers: this was Clare's concept of her mission. To be sure, the sisters of San Damiano had always been strangers—to themselves, first of all, and certainly in the world. But they were never pilgrims. Is this why the legs of Saint Clare became stone? To show the world that, even though enclosed, mutilated, and chained, they knew how to walk and go off on a holy pilgrimage by taking roads that were not earthly ones? Choosing streets paved with clouds and birds, on which legs are of much less use than a dragon-fly's wings?

I continue to cite from the Rule because its severity, typical of the period, manifests a level of attentiveness and care that is rare among women's communities. "If," Clare writes, "any sister, through the instigation of the enemy, shall have sinned mortally against the form of our profession, and if after having been admonished by the abbess or by other sisters, she will not amend, she shall eat bread and drink water while sitting on the floor before all the sisters in the refectory for as many days as she has been obstinate; and if it seems advisable to the abbess she shall undergo even greater punishment. Meanwhile, as long as she remains obstinate, let her pray that the Lord will enlighten her heart to do penance." These are strict words for dealing with those who have erred, even if they recommend reasoning with the sinner two or three times before resorting to punishment. Only if the young woman will not repent should she be humiliated in public. "The abbess and her sisters, however, must beware not to become angry or disturbed on account of anyone's sin: for anger and disturbance prevent charity in oneself and in others."

Evidently communal life was not always idyllic, as at times we might be led to believe. Even those who have dedicated themselves to God can harbor petty feelings, rancor, disrespect, bitterness—sentiments not always resolved through collective prayer. They wouldn't be human if this wasn't the case. But Clare didn't want to live in a barracks. She didn't want to live in a world dominated by rules, duties, and privations; she much preferred a close and harmonious community, whose members were there to help one another when in difficulty. It was more of a family than a college dormitory, more a home than a boarding school.

Given its deeply metaphorical language, the Bible was often invoked when articulating this project of freedom. It would seem contradictory that a blueprint for freedom could co-exist with severe constraints. But when a political plan is carefully chosen and forcefully defended, such extremes can be fused together, made one with your own flesh, so that every putrid stench is transformed into fragrance, every stone into a pillow, every blow into a caress. "Be very joyful and glad, filled with a remarkable happiness and a spiritual joy!" Clare writes to Agnes. "Because, since contempt of the world has pleased You more than its honors, poverty more than earthly riches, You have sought to store up greater treasures not on earth but in heaven, where rust does not consume nor moth destroy nor thieves break in and steal. Your reward is very rich in heaven! And You are virtually worthy to be called a sister, spouse, and mother of the Son of the Most High Father and of the glorious Virgin."

It seems obsessive, Clare's concern with poverty. And in fact, it was. We see her real genius in such a choice—her stubborn, marvelous passion for independence, even as she never renounced obedience, which she revered in the formal certainties it could provide. Tradition demanded distinctions and hierarchies: father and mother, son and daughter. The revolutionary liberty proposed by Clare turned these hierarchies on their head. In the act of liberation that followed, every father could become a mother, every son a husband, every daughter a sister and a mother.

Dear Author,
Don't think badly of me if I've just dropped in out of nowhere, after a long and shameful silence. I'm the one to blame. But I'm sure you won't have missed me. You've certainly had lots

to do with Clare of Assisi, and you won't have been thinking about that other Chiara, the Sicilian who watches you with trepidation from far away. Now that you've almost finished the book, can I start writing you again?

With much affection, CM

Dear Chiara,

You certainly have the knack of being able to surprise me. From what hole have you emerged? Why did you disappear in the first place? Most of all, why did you lie to me about your name and come up with a town that simply doesn't exist? And how did you ever figure out that I've almost finished the book? I don't understand your games of hide-and-seek, or your secretiveness, or your silence. Can you please tell me the truth about what's happened?

Dear Author,

So you still believe in truth? I stopped believing in it a long time ago. But whether you believe me or not, I'm very fond of you, and I'm back because I'm happy that you've become so passionate about my Clare. Do you know that this summer I went to Assisi for two months, guest of the nuns? And I've come to a decision with which I hope you'll agree: I'm going to become a Clarissa. I've already sent in my request and I'm hoping they'll take me in with them.

Dear Chiara,

Now I'm even more surprised. Though I wonder how you can become a nun if you don't believe in truth.

Dear Author,

I don't believe in the truths of this world. But I do believe in those of faith. Or rather I believe in the mystery that surrounds everything. That's why I like the idea of closing myself up in the convent. Even if today it seems almost anachronistic. Even if my parents think I'm crazy. Even if there's a part of me that protests. But I've heard Clare's voice. Not that she's called me—it would be too presumptuous of me to say that—but I heard her voice, gentle and kind, while she prayed in the chapel of San Damiano. I've seen the crucifix on which first Francis, then Clare, rested their gaze. That sallow and contorted figure enchanted me; maybe I've fallen in love with him, I'm not sure. Whatever I feel, it's overpowering. I don't know if this is about a true vocation. But from the moment I decided to enclose myself within, all my fears disappeared, along with my doubts, my uncertainties. Perhaps I didn't know who I was. Possibly I was looking for something I couldn't find in the wide streets of my city. While I've found it in the narrow streets of this little town.

Dear Chiara,
Since you're so accustomed to lying, why should I believe you now? If truth doesn't exist, then the world doesn't exist, my books don't exist, Italians don't exist, those bodies of Egyptians that at this very moment are lying covered with blood in Tahrir Square in Cairo, overwhelmed by the fury of a horrendous civil war, they don't exist. Are they only ghosts? Can you tell me once and for all who you are, and what you want from me?

Dear Author,
Don't take everything I say so literally. You'll never understand me. Maybe because I represent a part of yourself that you sensibly suppress because you're so anxious to explain everything and give every detail a name we can understand. You're a writer who tries to make reality tell a story. I'm a

restless girl who doesn't believe in facts—only in indecipherable feelings and extraordinary visions.

Dear Chiara,
You're very good at catching me off guard. What do you mean by "make reality tell a story"? Now I'm the one who's inventing the world! Incredible: I find myself talking to a Neoplatonist! But then it's possible that not even Clare of Assisi herself existed.

Dear Author,
I'm still that Sicilian girl who wrote you at the beginning of the year. The things I told you about my father and mother are all true. Only my town has a different name, and in any case I don't live there anymore. For years I've lived in a large city in the north. But I'd like you to imagine me among the dark rocks of Mount Etna. I've been trying to be a little unpredictable, like a flighty character who's dropped in from a fairy tale. I've never once lied to you. I've always been that girl who doesn't know who she is, who would like to have a happy body, who fasts out of desperation. Even if I feel better since I decided to enter the convent, as I've told you. I'm less anxious now, and I can even eat without having to make myself vomit. Your book has helped me enter into Clare's rooms. And I'm writing you from those very rooms, to tell you that this is the only possible choice for me right now, this choice of a life of silence and meditation. And I want to thank you for helping me make my decision.

Dear Chiara,
But how do you know these things about my writing when you haven't even read them? And what will a Sicilian girl who grew up on the slopes of Etna in a tiny village without

a name, a girl who suffers from insomnia and anorexia, whatever will she do in a convent in Assisi?

Dear Author,

You're not very good at using the computer, I can tell. I can see you, clumsy and self-conscious, sitting in front of your screen, ready to use it as though it were a piece of paper. You're too accustomed to your old Olivetti, Lettera 22, and have no idea of the infinite, even perverse capabilities of the machine right in front of your eyes. Of course there are programs that let you have access to other people's computers. Didn't you know that? All you have to do is learn how they work. All along I've been reading what you've been writing. As far as I'm concerned, you haven't dwelled all that much on the historical aspects, while I've enjoyed your descriptions of the convent of San Damiano. You've seen Clare and you've enabled us to see her in the flesh, in her bare feet—that's a nice thought, that the feet of someone who goes around without shoes would be covered with calluses—as she runs up and down in the convent. You've let us feel her humble mattress lying stiffly on the ground, the rock from the river she used for a pillow, her hands busily spinning and embroidering the altar covers she gave to the poor churches in her neighborhood, her hunger and diseases, her nightly visits to the chapel for prayer. I'm glad that you've also showed us her suffering and her misery, the life she chose for herself and nonetheless transformed into a path to freedom. That's it, I've liked everything you've done.

Still, I would have liked more, something more—I can't really tell you what I want. Presumptuously, perhaps, I would have wanted a capitulation, a total surrender to the reason and non-reason of faith. But I realize I'm asking too much. Yours is the simple heart of a thinker from the Enlightenment, and it guides you and shapes you. You're too attached to arguing and understanding to know how to lose yourself in something. And faith demands complete abandon.

Dear Chiara,

Don't change the subject, please. What does my "Enlightenment heart" have to do with any of this? And it's outrageous that you accessed my computer, that you've read everything I've been writing, that you've burrowed into my words. Doesn't this seem arrogant and indiscreet, even punishable by law? And here I was thinking you'd disappeared off into the fog of an island that doesn't exist. I thought that *you* were a creature who had never existed. Instead, I find out you're a con artist, an imposter, a thief of others' thoughts. How can you have permitted yourself to spy on me in this way?

Dear Author,

You don't need to be angry. I've done everything out of love and good faith. I was the one who pushed you toward Clare in the first place. Don't I have the right to know if you continued to follow my suggestions or if you'd stopped and gone on to think about something else? Didn't I have the right to linger discretely at your side, without disturbing you, to make sure that you did your job until it was finished? If I didn't respect you, I wouldn't have done it. I'm glad that from an epistolary novel you went on to writing a diary, in the tradition of women's literature. Moreover, I swear that I've never rifled through your emails, I've never nosed around in your letters. I've only followed your itinerary to Assisi. You say at one point that there is no corresponding word for "fraternal." But there is, and it's "sororal." I feel "sororal" when I'm speaking to you, I really do.

With much affection, Chiara

Dear Chiara,

Yes, I do seem to have run into that word. In his preface to Chiara Cremaschi's book, Cesare Vaiani says he was pleasantly surprised by her project, speaking of "the decisive and conscious feminine perspective with which her argument was carried out." He admires "the recurrent use of the substantive 'sorority' and the related adjective 'sororal' as equivalents for the male fraternity and fraternal," noting that she exhibits a "clear attachment to a language of inclusiveness that is employed infrequently in Italy, but is widespread in countries where English is spoken." And he adds that it's not just a question of words, since it "also reveals an awareness of the difference gender makes for every human experience." But to come back to your unspeakable indiscretion, I ask you: isn't it forbidden to access other people's computers?

Dear Author,

It's illegal if you do it without their permission, but if someone gives their consent, then it's okay. You might not remember, but I once asked you what books you'd found on Clare, and when you told me you had a long list on a file on your desktop, I suggested that we utilize a program that would let me access your computer via a password provided by the program itself. You agreed and gave me permission to have remote control of your desktop so I could copy that long list of books on Clare and the Middle Ages. I told you I would cancel the password as soon as I'd finished copying the list. Do you remember that? But I didn't cancel it. With your consent I logged back on to your computer as a guest, and I never went away. I simply did what you write about in your book *Colomba*: I'm that character who knocks at the door, enters, and asks for tea. Then in the evening I ask for supper and a bed to sleep in. As you wrote yourself, "This is the moment when I understand that I have to start writing the novel." I didn't commit a crime. I'm only following a procedure laid out by you, and I've followed it to the letter. However, I'm sorry I didn't tell you about it. I beg you, I beseech you to forgive me. I didn't want to offend you, I only wanted to follow your every step, to peek at what you were writing and satisfy this passion that has culminated in being able to see through Clare's own eyes. I confess all this with a certain pride, but without any malice: I only wanted to be close to you throughout this undertaking—one that has excited and moved me.

Dear Chiara,

What you're telling me seems crazy. However, it's true, I did give you permission once to access my computer. I remember now, and so it's my fault. I thought the password would be good just that one time and then it would expire. Instead, you tricked me. Does it seem right to take advantage of my lack of familiarity with technology?

Dear Author,

I'm sorry I fooled you. But I believe that the end justifies the means. Just what Cardinal Ugolino thought, who then became Pope Gregory IX. That's what the Church has always thought. And I must tell you that although my rational little soul rejects him, I agree with Innocent III. I place my trust in good faith and in good ends. An end that must be honest and just, otherwise it's simply a question of fraud. I don't believe I swindled you. If that little trick of technology was the only way to get you to write about Clare, then my deception was justified. The rules don't stop those of us who are thirsty for good stories.

Okay, so now can we get back to your book? I'm especially struck by your insistence on Clare's illness. If she was so good at healing babies and nuns, how come she was never able to cure her own paralysis? If I'm not mistaken, you find something symbolic in the fact that her legs became numb. Almost as though the prohibition to go forth and preach and carry out what Francis had envisioned for her—and what many other religious women were doing in Europe back then—awakened in Clare a protest that enforced the opposite. As if her condemnation to immobility and seclusion trapped her body within a marmoreal silence. But at the same time, it gave wings to her imagination as she ran behind Francis, carried by his strong legs throughout Italy and the world preaching the word of Christ. Am I reading you correctly? I have to say that I too have asked myself where that crippling sickness came from that confined her to bed for so many years. From the time she was thirty until she was fifty-nine, an eternity. Clare fell ill in exactly the same year that Francis received the stigmata. Is there any significance in that detail, or is it mere coincidence? However, I must say that I don't like this constant interrogation of the sacred. We must approach the holy in silence and acceptance.

Dear Chiara,
You're pretending that nothing has happened, but I'm still angry at you. There's something diabolical about what you did, and I find no justification in your concern that I write about Clare. After all, as I told you the first time I wrote you, the metaphor of the character who comes to knock at my door works only if the character speaks in his own voice. Not through third parties, as you've done. There's a great deal of impudence in all this knocking on doors on someone else's behalf. A great deal of arrogance and insolence in the

pretext that I'm telling a story that has nothing to do with you save for the coincidence of your name. I'm tempted to cut off this correspondence, I have to tell you with all sincerity.

Nonetheless I'm still writing you; despite my indignation, my hands are still at the keyboard. It must mean that in my mind I've already forgiven you. Something tells me there's a kernel of necessity in your deceit. And at heart I can't help but be grateful to you for having put me in touch with this extraordinary woman, even though she's been dead for centuries. I can't help but be grateful to you for having forced me to read book after book about Saint Francis, about one pope after another, about the high Middle Ages, about literature written in Provençal and Occitan, for having forced me to read up on the history of convents and monastic life.

Dear Author,

I'm so grateful you forgave me that I'm jumping for joy. In my stubborn little Sicilian head I'm hopping up and down like a kangaroo. Have you ever seen a kangaroo jump? It's one of the funniest sights you can imagine—yet also poetic, and sweet. Once I went to Australia with some friends. We were all young, all penniless. We had grabbed a last-minute discount and set off, ready to make do with whatever we found. It wasn't easy: we stayed in hostels overflowing with teenagers, sleeping one next to the other on bunk beds inside dusty classrooms, eating dry sea biscuits and drinking black tea with no sugar. My favorite memory—other than seeing the enormous cultural center, a theatre built to look like a seafaring vessel with lovely white sails—is from our trip into the hinterlands, the region of Coonawarra or the "redlands," with its killer wasps and kangaroos. We went around with nets over our heads so we wouldn't get stung. I never saw so many wasps in my life. They arrived in hordes and targeted our faces, as though they wanted to suck on them like honeycomb. I finally saw kangaroos hopping about, and I can assure you that it was an amazing sight. A quadruped that doesn't walk around on its four paws—what's that about? Such a strange beast: two robust legs in the back with feet like shovels, and in the front two tiny, malformed arms with paws for eating, cradling their young, uprooting plants. Well, that's how I'm feeling today. And my heart is singing. Or as Bruce Chatwin might say, the streets of the Australian Aboriginals are singing. My hands are singing, my eyes, my hair. And everything inside me is leaping about to the rhythm of the kangaroo. Thank you.

Dear Clare,

Let's not exaggerate with all this gratitude; it's embarrassing. I've been to Australia too. Like you, I've admired the architectural sails of the Opera House. I also thought kangaroos were strange creatures—although I didn't see too many of them. I think they're disappearing, like all wildlife. We're destroying them with deforestation, as we dry up the rivers and throw cement everywhere: in other words, with our systematic slaughter of everything that is most beautiful.

But let's get back to Clare. When you started to write me again, I was in the middle of tackling a subject that interested me. Many of the witnesses for her canonization speak of the contempt that Lady Clare had for her own body, as well as for herself as a person. When the judge asked Suor Beatrice how she would define Clare's qualities, she answered, "Clare's holiness consisted in her humility, her patience and kindness, in the necessary correction and sweet chastising of her sisters, in her persistent prayer and contemplation, in abstinence and fasting, in the austerity of her sleeping conditions and her dress, in her contempt [*despresso*] for herself, in the fervor of her love for God, in her desire for martyrdom, and especially in her love for the privilege of poverty." So, the question I ask myself is this: Can one really have contempt for oneself? Or is the word *despresso* here, rather than indicating contempt, describing a way of making yourself small in front of others out of modesty and reserve? Can you be patient, sweet, and gentle with others if you don't value yourself? It's a question I've been pondering and for which I have no answer.

Dear Author,

As far as I can tell, this *despresso* of which Suor Beatrice speaks is really forgetfulness of oneself. I think Clare wanted to demonstrate the practice of serving others, the joy of giving herself. I don't think you should say she was contemptuous of herself. As you rightly note, you can't love someone if you don't hold yourself in esteem. But denigrating oneself back then was almost a duty, I would say a spiritual necessity.

Dear Clare,

Is it possible to desire martyrdom? This too is something I've wondered about and that I asked myself while I was writing. If I understand it correctly, it means that you take pleasure in pain. Is that what this woman of faith sought for her imprisoned body? If you love someone who has been tortured, is it permissible to want to torture your own body? Is it truly a sign of love, or just a way of imitating love? Up to what point is it permissible to punish one's own flesh out of love? Isn't love about desiring the good of the other? But doesn't the pleasure of pain end by being transformed into its opposite? That is, in desiring the good of the other, you want to incorporate into yourself the very evils the other has suffered. Is this sublimated love? Doesn't it seem to entail a compulsion to repeat? I ask myself if this compulsion wasn't a perverse product of the religious totalitarianism of the Middle Ages, rather than a new version of divine love. Isn't a religion that seeks to mortify life itself much too cruel? Could we say that this poison of self-hatred, self-contempt, self-torture, still runs in the veins of women who, in the absence of any totalitarian regime, continue to call up the pleasures of suffering out of blind obedience to the history of their sex?

Dear Author,

I think you're seeing things from the wrong perspective. Deriving pleasure from pain purely for erotic reasons—as certain trendy books would suggest these days—is the work of the devil. But to want to absorb into one's own body the suffering and torture that Christ experienced is a profoundly generous act of love. This is what led Clare to wear a rough hair shirt made from horsehair, to lie on an uncomfortable sack of straw and a pillow of stone. Nowadays, finding pleasure in pain is a form of perversity that is an end in itself; I realize that. And it's widespread among women. Eros is in there somewhere, but it doesn't want to come out and liberate itself.

The persistence throughout history of such a compulsion doesn't justify anything. Do we want to call it masochism? In the harsh Middle Ages, the one-dimensional Middle Ages—wasn't three dimensionality Galileo's discovery?—the love of pain was something else; it was tolerated, it was intelligible. Don't you think that concepts such as love, motherhood, virginity, freedom, are better understood when we study the cultural realities in which they're rooted, rather than seeing them as mere commonplaces? It feels dangerous to me to judge Clare with today's eyes. We must accept her in all her mystery, with all her contradictions. Which weren't contradictions when she was alive, but rather ways of attaching oneself to reality. If we want to get close to her, we have to understand the enormous obstacles she faced—obstacles she overcame thanks to her ironclad fidelity to her own principles, which never turned into stubbornness, rancor, hatred, violence, fanaticism. That's rare among nonconformists who want to impose their vision of the world onto others. It's something Clare paid for with her very flesh, this fidelity that has moved people and moves us still. At a time when people talk about and indulge in infidelity with complete nonchalance, Clare's obstinate constancy can still teach us something. She provides an extraordinary example. I feel that and want you to feel that way too.

Dear Chiara,

Since you've decided to enter the convent, you've left your challenges and uncertainties behind. I don't know if this makes things better or worse for you. As far as I'm concerned, it's a real loss. I can't think when I'm wearing blinders, and I don't understand why in today's world the act of shutting oneself up behind a grate doesn't constitute an act of cruelty against oneself.

Dear Author,

Once again you're making a mistake by prioritizing reason over deep thought, verisimilitude over the gift of oneself. My vocation—can we call it that?—isn't a voluntary choice. It doesn't proceed by calculating gains and losses. Listen to these beautiful lines by Leopardi: "Thus in such / immensity my thoughts are drowned: / and to be shipwrecked in this sea is sweet." I have no other answer for you.

But I'd like you to finish writing the book. I don't want to be popping up at your window before you're ready. The story still needs a conclusion. How did Clare die, and when? I know what happens, but I want you to tell me.

Dear Chiara,

You're right—I haven't finished the book, because you interrupted me. Maybe it's true, you showed up too soon at my window and I wasn't expecting it, especially with that trick of yours that caught me off guard. Turn to Clare's death? But do you know that since you started writing me again, I've no longer been dreaming about her? The manner in which she approaches her end is very pure, very serious, very self-aware. Clare is lying on a wooden bed, or so it would seem from the earliest drawings and paintings we have of her. As her disease progressed and they started fearing the worst, the sisters lifted her up from her pallet on the floor and prepared for her a real bed, a wooden one, with woven blankets and a pillow stuffed with feathers and no longer one of stone.

Witnesses say that Clare was waiting for the bull of Pope Innocent IV to arrive and ratify her testament, her *Forma Vitae*. Who knows what it cost her to wait—and she'd already been waiting for years! She knew she was dying, but she didn't want to go before the bull was confirmed. She couldn't imagine that as soon as she was gone they would change the very things she had requested. In fact, by making her a saint they deprived her of all responsibility for her own will and testament.

The nuns were "seated alongside the bed of their lady, in tears," gathered for her final suffering. She lay motionless before them, her eyes closed; she seemed already to be dead, but she was still breathing. No one dared address her, when suddenly they heard her voice, light and clear. They couldn't believe their ears. It was as though life had been reborn in this body without strength, this body of their abbess. "Go in peace because you will have a good guide," says the voice, very clearly, "since he who created you foresaw that you would be sanctified, having infused you with the Holy Spirit when you were born, and he has protected you just as a mother protects her little child." Suor Anastasia leaned over and asked her in a hushed voice to whom she was speaking. And Clare answered, "I'm speaking to my blessed soul."

When we listen to these words of Suor Anastasia, we can tell that Clare did not, in fact, disdain herself. Indeed, she was perfectly aware of her worth, certain she would be assumed into heaven. But at the same time, we know that Clare was in the habit of talking to herself, or to her soul. And so it's likely it was her soul that told her that her wait was over, that the mortifications and physical sufferings she had inflicted on herself all those years were at an end, and that for once she could abandon herself to the pleasure of being cared for by the Holy Spirit in the same way a mother cares for her beloved child.

Dear Author,
I'm delighted that you've picked up the story line again. At this point I'll get myself out of the picture. Please, continue your narration. But you should mention something that Suor Anastasia said in her testimony, and that Suor Benvenuta de Madonna Diambra de Assisi told the judges as well. Anastasia saw the entire court of heaven getting ready to welcome "the dying, holy mother"—isn't that true? And she maintains that the Virgin Mary herself "was preparing the garments in which to clothe this new bride."

Dear Chiara,

Where do you go each time? You seem to be the cat in *Alice in Wonderland*, appearing and vanishing like a sprite. You don't laugh like the cat in *Alice*, but you do smile, never giving away your thoughts. There's something mysterious about you that I still don't understand. Besides, you yourself said that you wanted to stay out of things and not be like a flighty interlocutor from a fairy tale. What other surprises might I expect from you?

Dear Author,

Please, just continue as though I weren't here. I don't want to be flighty and mysterious, but discreet and uninvolved. I'll follow you from far off. Start with Suor Benvenuta who saw the Virgin Mary come into the room when Clare was dying so she could dress her in her bridal gown. I beg you!

Dear Clare,

"She prepared the garments in which to clothe this new bride": that's what Suor Benvenuta says. So you want me to take up the subject of the wedding. It certainly is comforting to imagine that a body as it dies is not destroyed, is not about to rot away, but is being readied to meet its bridegroom in great splendor, dressed in solemn new clothes—the groom Clare has waited for her whole life. Suor Benvenuta had a very detailed vision: "Above her head she held a crown, and above the crown was a vessel for incense in the shape of a golden apple, which emitted such fragrance that it seemed to permeate the entire house." Behind the bed of her abbess she saw a troupe of virgins approach, all dressed in white, "with crowns upon their heads as well." Are these the other brides of Christ who have come to welcome the new arrival?

Rituals are always spectacular. Benvenuta sees the Virgin Mary approaching the bed of the dying woman. She bends over her sweetly, "leaning over the face of the aforementioned virgin Saint Clare, or more precisely, over her bosom." From far away she couldn't make out whether it was her face or her breast, but the nun clearly sees Mary leaning over Clare and giving her a kiss. The judge asked her if she had been asleep, perhaps dreaming. And Benvenuta said no, she was wide awake. The judge insists: But were you alone? Weren't there other nuns with you? What did the others see? Benvenuta answers that other nuns were indeed present, but some of them had dozed off, while others were awake, but she didn't know if they'd seen exactly what she did. Not everyone gets to see a miracle.

Clare didn't want to die before she knew what was happening with the papal bull that had been promised her and for which she had been waiting for years. But instead of sending the bull, the pope himself went to meet her: Innocent IV in person, in his magnificent robes, with his elegant retinue. It was July, and extremely hot. The nuns turned the convent upside down to get it ready for the Holy Father. They spent that morning in late July cleaning and polishing the floors of the chapel, the *parlatorio*, the dormitory. They cleaned off the rim of the well with its thick, dank, rotting grass. They offered the holy father wine mixed with honey along with biscotti baked by one of the nuns, using the flour that peasants had brought to the convent along with two little bags of salt and a handful of onions as soon as they'd learned about the distinguished visitor. They also placed a vase of flowers next to Clare's bed.

"And Messer Pope Innocent came to visit her when she was gravely ill," recounts Suor Philippa. What did the pope say, and what did Clare say? The nuns didn't divulge anything at the trial, but it's plausible to think that Clare asked for papal approval for her *Forma Vitae* for which she had fought so strenuously. And from Clare's joy, one can only assume that he promised to sign the famous, long-awaited papal bull. "Lady Clare then said to the nuns: 'My daughters, praise God, because heaven and earth are not enough to contain all of the goodness I've received from God, for today I received him in the holy Sacrament, and I have also seen his Vicar.'"

Nonetheless, others maintain that the pope did not go to see Clare just a few days before she died in late July, but that he went much earlier, in May, and that Clare had wanted to get up to kiss not only his hand, but his foot. Since she couldn't stand, the pope requested that a stool be brought over, on which he placed his foot so she could kiss it. In the Middle Ages dates weren't very important, as Sister Chiara Giovanna Cremaschi suggests. The key thing is that the pope went to visit the ailing woman. Suor Philippa herself, when interrogated by the judge as to "how long before the death of this Lady Clare the visit took place, answered, 'A few days.'"

The pope *did* send the bull, furnished with his official signature, and it arrived two days before Clare died. "And this lady was greatly desirous to have the rule sealed with the bull, so that one day she could hold it to her lips, and then the next day she could die," says Suor Philippa, who among all the witnesses is the most precise, the most thorough, the most detailed. "And it happened just as she'd hoped. For a friar arrived with the sealed letters, which she reverently received even though she was so close to death, and she herself brought that seal to her mouth to kiss it." And the next day, she died: "The following day, the aforementioned Lady Clare passed from this life to her Lord: she who is truly luminous, without stain, without the shadow of sin passed into the clarity of eternal light."

There are many who have played on the various meanings of the name Clare, including her own sisters: *Chiara, clara, clarando, clarità, clamore*: light, luminous, lightening, clarity, clamor. Legend has it that when her mother Ortolana was pregnant, she went to church to pray, "and standing before the cross and concentrating on her prayer, she asked God to be with her and to assist her in the dangers of childbirth." She heard a voice coming from the crucifix that said, "You will give birth to a light that will illuminate the whole world." Once again, these are the words of Suor Philippa.

AUGUST 24. The month is almost over, and I have to turn in my book to my editor. I've never worked so hard, without resting for even an hour, going from 6:30 in the morning to 8 at night. I break only for meals, for a walk at noon and another at 6:30. It's true, I hunkered down one other time like this, when Pier Paolo Pasolini and I wrote the screenplay for *The Flower of a Thousand and One Nights*. I don't know why Pier Paolo got the idea in his head to finish the screenplay in fifteen days; maybe his contract forced him to do it that quickly, as though he had a noose around his neck. He had read my *Memoir of a Lady Thief* and enjoyed its picaresque style, so he asked me to help him tell the story of Zummurud, the shrewd female slave. That's why we locked ourselves up in a house in Sabaudia, on the ocean. But I never even glimpsed the sea. I only smelled it at night when it would send forth its devastating perfumes mixed with salt and algae. We worked at a feverish pitch, twelve hours a day, interrupting ourselves only for a light meal and starting up again immediately afterwards, until nightfall. I recall our immense, almost inhuman effort, leaving no time for a swim in the sea, or a walk, or a second to breathe. But it was also a period of intimacy and intense concentration.

I'm sorry that Chiara Mandalà has vanished once again. Who knows if it's true that she's enclosed herself in a convent; who knows if she'll ever write me again. I don't even know if she'll read the book when it comes out. But she's already done everything she could: she led me by the hand into this ancient, tragic, and beautiful story; she followed me, she spied on me, she guided me, and then she took off without leaving a trace. I don't know whether I should thank her or be upset with her for having made me work so hard.

But Saint Clare hasn't taken her final breath just yet. She's still stretched out on her deathbed. After a long silence it seems that she wants to break the rules and speak: "And at the end of her life, she called to her side all of her sisters and fervently urged them to observe the Privilege of Poverty." That was what she held to most fiercely. She repeated it again and again, often citing the words of Francis: "Where there is poverty and joy, there is neither avarice nor greed," as he writes in his *Admonitions*. And again, as he said in the Rule of 1221: "The brothers and ministers of the friars should prevent themselves from engaging in any way in their own interests, nor should they receive any money for themselves or through the intervention of others." And still more: "No friar, no matter where he is or where he is going, is allowed to carry with him, or to accept or have accepted for him money in any way or in any form, not even if it is for purposes of procuring clothing or books or received as wages. For we must be convinced that money is no more useful or valuable than stones. Whoever desires and values money more than stones has been blinded by the devil." And finally: "If for some reason, God forbid, it happens that some friar collect or retain money that is permitted only for the needs of the ill, the other friars will consider him fraudulent, a thief and an assassin and a hoarder of goods, unless he sincerely repents."

So coins are as worthless as stones. And whoever imagines that stones could ever be important is not only deluded, but a murderer and a thief. That's what Clare thought as well. The women who chose to join her convent were supposed to scorn stones that ordinary people use for buying things, for making themselves powerful and arrogant. Money was alien to the convent, along with bargaining, making contracts, negotiating. No guarantees, no certainties, no insurance for the future. One simply lived day by day. Such willingness to submit to the vagaries of chance offended the powerful. Radical and subversive as it was, Clare's conviction was rooted in an egalitarian, anarchic idea of liberty that knew no bounds—and that could never be acceptable to anyone in authority.

"Let the nuns, serving the Lord in humility and poverty, send out with confidence for alms," prescribes Clare in her Rule. Not only were you allowed to ask for alms; you *had* to ask for them. And this was nothing to be ashamed of. "Let us remember that our Lord Jesus Christ, son of the living and omnipotent God, set his face like flint and was not ashamed." Those are the words of Francis. "And he was poor and had no home and he lived on alms, along with the Blessed Virgin and his disciples. Should men shame them and refuse to give them alms, they should thank God, because they will receive great honor before the tribunal of our Lord Jesus Christ. Let it be known that shame will be imputed not to those who suffer it, but to those who cause it. Alms are an inheritance and a right owed to the poor, acquired for us by our Lord Jesus Christ."

Bold thoughts, analyzed as we have seen by Agamben; Clare and Francis did not consider almsgiving to be an act of generosity that bore witness to a good heart, but a right given by the Lord to the weakest and most indigent. This right wouldn't sit well with the authorities of the Holy See, because it sounded too revolutionary—this right to "most exalted poverty," as Clare would call it. A poverty that "has rendered you, my dearest sisters, the heiresses and queens of the kingdom of Heaven, poor in substance, but sublime in virtue."

Pope Innocent IV, who held Clare in great esteem because of her "odor of sanctity," because of the prestige she enjoyed among the faithful and her growing popularity that enabled the Church to shine all the more brightly, was already engaged in generating a new Rule that would be applicable to all convents. Monastic communities, especially women's, had too much autonomy and were poorly run. And thus the very thing that Clare most prized, absolute and radical poverty, would be overturned by the "right"—effectively, the obligation—to own earthly goods, possessions as well as land. In order to support the enclosed nuns, of course.

"You are allowed to accept and hold revenues and property in common, and to freely maintain them," says the New Rule that oversaw all female convents. "In order to administer your goods, each of your monasteries will have a prudent and trustworthy procurer. The procurer, lawfully nominated, is required to be accountable for everything entrusted to him as recorded in the entry books of the abbess." We might say that this sounds logical and sensible, but it's a matter of a "prescriptive" Rule, as Paolo Scandaletti argues in his book on Clare. Above all, it eliminated the requirement of absolute poverty demanded by the saint. The procurer, or the administrator, would do nothing but intervene, count, control, and regulate what goes into the convent and what goes out. So it is that money—those stones so hated and scorned by Francis—was thrown out the front door, only to come back in through the window.

AUGUST 26. I'm so tired that like an idiot I tripped in a ravine, slipping on some pine cones while I was walking in the woods behind the cemetery of Pescasseroli. As if for a moment I'd fallen asleep while taking a walk. I whacked my chest and my leg, and now I'm limping and full of aches and pains. I may have broken a rib on my left side. But I can't stop now. I have to deliver the book as promised. My stupid sense of obligation has me all tied up in knots. Chiara Mandalà, where are you, with your wisdom of a fanatic, your flattery, your tenacity of a wolf? Without realizing it, I've started addressing you in the informal mode, the *tu* of invective. Does one's consciousness exult when confronted with deprivation and trials, or is it weakened? Up to what point is it fair to force our creative energies to express themselves? Up to what point should you egg on your imagination when it's tired, when all it wants to do is to spread out beneath the shade of a tree?

In her beautiful letter to Agnes of Bohemia, Clare writes:

O blessed poverty!
To all who love and embrace you,
you offer eternal riches! O holy poverty,
the kingdom of heaven,
eternal glory and a blessed life
are surely granted
to all who obey and desire you!
O pious poverty,
which our Lord Jesus Christ, who governs
heaven and earth and governs them still,
our Lord who spoke and everything was created:

he deemed you worthy of his embrace,
preferring you above all others.

Even animals crave a sense of security. You're allowed to want to have a roof over your head, but not to consider it property, because property is vanity. For a society dominated by the market such as our own, what sense can these words possibly have? As the Gospel of Matthew reminds us, "The foxes have holes, and the birds of the air have their nests, but the Son of man has nowhere to lay his head."

Is it possible to envision a way for a philosophy of privation to guide us when thinking about the relationship between the sexes? If we could follow Clare's directions and challenge the assumption that love gives one the right to possess another, that would be a promising start. Clare certainly never intended to put her love for poverty in these terms, but the truth of what she said transcends her own time, as is the case for the words of other major figures. And her truths are so revolutionary that they can inspire us to banish any form of ownership that's routine or disrespectful, carnal or erotic. What a refreshing antidote that would be today, with all our neuroses about the things we possess, and the things we consume.

Dear Author,
I don't know how to express my gratitude. I know you've done an enormous amount of work. I hope you're not still sick and that your ribs have healed. I feel a little guilty for having dragged you into this, but I hope it was worth the effort. I fell in love with Clare, so much so that I followed her into the convent. And I thank you for that. Only now do I think I understand what it means to have a body that's

happy. I won't confine my breasts within a cord made from horse hair, and I won't tie a girdle lined with pigskin around my waist. But I'll sing in church, where finally my voice can take on wings. I'll sleep in a modest, narrow bed, not on the ground and not on a sack filled with straw or vine shoots. I won't be using a rock from the river for my pillow. I won't have to chase the fleas out from under the covers—I'll have sheets, and I won't consider them diabolical temptations. Nor will I think of the devil as a spider with sticky paws, as Saint Catherine once did. Something of the interior force of Clare and her sisters will continue to flow through these rooms that haven't yet forgotten the tenacity and joyous warmth of those nuns. Maybe I've learned that the body can practice chastity without subjecting itself to torture. We can be chaste from the sheer joy of love.

Notes on the Translation
and References

All translations from the Italian are my own, with the exception of the passage from *Pinocchio*, translated by Carol Della Chiesa (New York: Macmillan, 1929). As for English translations from the Latin texts of and about Clare and Francis: for Clare's Rule, *Francis and Clare: The Complete Works*, translation and introduction by Regis J. Armstrong and Ignatius C. Brady (New York: Paulist Press, 1982); for Bonaventure's *Legenda maior, Francis of Assisi: Early Documents*, vol. 2, edited by Regis J. Armstrong, J. A. Wayne Hellmann, and William J. Short (Hyde Park, NY: New City Press, 1999–2002); for Clare's letters to Agnes, *The Lady Clare of Assisi: Early Documents*, edited and translated by Regis J. Armstrong (New York: New City Press, 2006). The latter text also contains a full English translation of the Acts of Canonization.

All biblical passages are from *The Oxford Study Bible* (New York: Oxford University Press, 1970). The passages from the Passion of Perpetua are my own, but see Peter Dronke, *Women Writers of the Middle Ages: A Critical Study of Texts from Perpetua (203) to Marguerite Porete (1310)* (Cambridge: Cambridge University Press, 1984). I have used the English translation of the five-volume work, originally in French, *History of Women in the West*, edited by Georges Duby and

Michelle Perrot (Cambridge, MA: Harvard University Press, 1992), for the several essays quoted by Maraini throughout, all from volume 2 (*Silences of the Middle Ages*). Clarissa Botsford translated the essays by Silvana Vecchio, Carla Casagrande, and Chiara Frugoni; Arthur Goldhammer translated the essays by Françoise Piponnier and Paulette L'Hermite-Leclercq.

Many of the women mystics whom Maraini cites can be found in the collection *Scrittrici mistiche italiane*, edited by Giovanni Pozzi and Claudio Leonardi (Geneva: Marietti, 2004). More than a few of them have had their works translated into English in the last two decades, thanks to the series edited by Margaret King and Albert Rabil Jr., *The Other Voice in Early Modern Europe*, based with Iter Press.

Other works that the author cites in her text and/or lists in her bibliography include:

Agamben, Giorgio. *Altissima povertà: Regole monastiche e forma di vita*. Vicenza: Neri Pozza, 2011.

Bargellini, Piero. *I Fioretti di Santa Chiara*. Assisi: Porziuncola, 2007.

Block, Marc. *Feudal Society*. London: Routledge, 2014.

Boccali, Giovanni, ed. *Santa Chiara d'Assisi sotto processo: Lettura storica spirituale degli atti di canonizzazione*. Assisi: Porziuncola, 2003.

———. *Tutti gli scritti di San Francesco e Santa Chiara d'Assisi*. Assisi: Porziuncola, 2011.

Cardini, Franco. *Francesco d'Assisi*. Milan: Mondadori, 1997.

———. *In Terrasanta: Pellegrini italiani tra Medioevo e prima età moderna*. Bologna: Il Mulino, 2005.

Chevalier, Jean, and Alain Gheerbrant. *Dizionario dei simboli: Miti, sogni, costumi, gesti, forme, figure, colori, numeri*. Milan: Biblioteca Universale Rizzoli, 2004.

Cremaschi, Chiara Giovanna. *Chiara d'Assisi: Un silenzio che grida.* Assisi: Porziuncola, 2008.

Delort, Robert. *La vita quotidiana nel Medioevo.* Bari: Laterza, 2009.

De Matteis, Maria Consiglia, ed. *Donne nel Medioevo: Aspetti culturali e di vita quotidiana. Antologia di scritti.* Bologna: Patron, 1986.

Evangelisti, Silvia. *Storia delle Monache.* Bologna: Il Mulino, 2012.

Frugoni, Chiara. *Una solitudine abitata: Chiara d'Assisi.* Bari: Laterza, 2006.

———. *Storia di Chiara e Francesco.* Turin: Einaudi, 2011.

Laven, Mary. *Virgins of Venice: Enclosed Lives and Broken Vows in the Renaissance Convent.* London: Viking, 2002.

Le Goff, Jacques. *Il basso medioevo.* Milan: Feltrinelli, 1989.

Origo, Iris. *The Merchant of Prato: Francesco di Marco Datini, 1335–1410.* New York: Penguin, 2020.

Pognon, Edmund. *La vita quotidiana nell'anno Mille.* Milan: Biblioteca Universale Rizzoli, 1989.

Power, Eileen. *Medieval People.* New York: Dover, 2000 [1924].

Scandaletti, Paolo. *Chiara d'Assisi.* Milan: Biblioteca Universale Rizzoli, 2002.

Tommaso da Celano. *Vita di S Chiara vergine d'Assisi.* Translated by Fausta Casolini. Assisi: Porziuncola, 2002.

Vaiani, Cesare. *Francesco e Chiara d'Assisi.* Milan: Glossa, 2004.

Notes on Contributors

DACIA MARAINI is one of Italy's most pre-eminent and beloved writers. She is the daughter of ethnologist Fosco Maraini and Topazia Alliata di Salaparuta, a painter and Sicilian aristocrat. Born in Fiesole, at eighteen she moved to Rome, where she met and began collaborating with important intellectual figures such as Alberto Moravia, Pier Paolo Pasolini, and the members of the neo-avant-garde movement Gruppo 63 (Group 63). In 1973 she founded the Teatro delle Maddalene, dedicated to works by women; she has written over thirty plays, among which *Maria Stuarda* and *Dialogo di una Prostituta con un suo Cliente* have acquired international fame. Previous novels include a thriller about a female detective, *Voci* (Voices) and the international bestseller *La Lunga Vita di Marianna Ucrìa* (The Silent Duchess). She also writes a weekly column for Italy's best-selling newspaper, *Corriere della Sera*.

JANE TYLUS is Andrew Downey Orrick Professor of Italian and Comparative Literature at Yale University; she held prior appointments at NYU and the University of Wisconsin–Madison. Recent books include *Siena, City of Secrets*, the co-edited *Cultures of Early Modern Translation* (with Karen Newman), and the translation of the complete poetry of Gaspara Stampa, Italy's finest female poet. She won the MLA prize for *Reclaiming Catherine of Siena* and the Outstanding Translation Prize from the Society for the Study of Early Modern Women for her translation of the poetry of Lucrezia Tornabuoni de'Medici. She has appeared with Dacia Maraini in venues in Florence, Rome, London, Cambridge (England), New Haven, and New York.